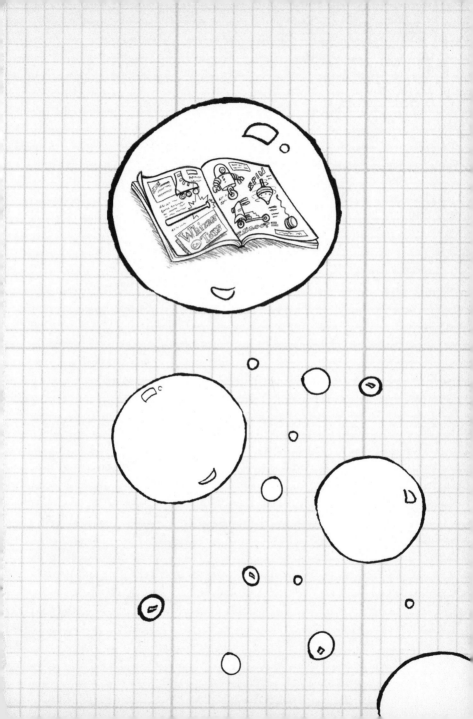

Interior and Invention
notebook illustrations by
GUY FRANCIS

Invention notebook
design by
**OLIVE AND
COMPANY**

★ Vincent Shadow ★
The TOP SECRET Toys

by Tim Kehoe

LITTLE, BROWN AND COMPANY
New York Boston

Little, Brown and Company

Hachette Book Group
237 Park Avenue, New York, NY 10017
Visit our website at www.lb-kids.com

Little, Brown and Company is a division of Hachette Book Group, Inc.
The Little, Brown name and logo are trademarks of Hachette Book Group, Inc.

The publisher is not responsible for websites (or their content)
that are not owned by the publisher.

First Edition: February 2012

ISBN 978-0-316-05669-4

10 9 8 7 6 5 4 3 2 1

RRD-C

Printed in the United States of America

Book design by Saho Fujii

The text and the display type were set in Eurocrat.

AUTHOR'S NOTE:

This book is a **work of fiction** and intended **solely for reading entertainment.** It is not intended to be a guidebook for any of the experiments or activities described in this book. **The experiments and activities described in this book can be extremely dangerous** and the reader should not attempt to recreate them. Before doing *any* kind of science experiment, readers are advised to **ask a responsible adult about the dangers** that may be involved and, with the help of that adult, take the necessary precautions. The author and publisher disclaim any liability that is incurred from the application of the contents of this book.

BUNK BEDS

1

New York, New York

All parents keep a secret list of mistakes
—a top-secret list of regrets that they share only with other parents. And while some of those lists may include the purchase of bunk beds, Nancy Zimmerman is, perhaps, the only parent to put the purchase of her son's bunk bed at the very top of the list.

Timmy Zimmerman, better known as Danger Boy

to his friends and family, discovered his love of stunts shortly after his mother purchased his bunk bed. The bed had played a major role in many of his death-defying stunts over the years. But today Timmy was preparing to take danger to a new level.

Timmy carefully removed the plastic motorcycle models from his bookcase and leaned the empty bookcase against his bunk bed. Then he positioned his bike jump at the base of the bookcase. Now the back of the bookcase formed a solid ramp to the bike jump.

Timmy duct-taped a pillow to his old skateboard and climbed to the top bunk. He looked down the ramp and figured he would be traveling thirty or fifty miles per hour by the time he reached the jump. Professional stuntmen always take safety precautions and Timmy believed he was nothing if not professional. So he strapped on his foam bike helmet and mounted the skateboard.

Timmy was lying headfirst on the skateboard. A simple push would propel him down the ramp, over the jump and, if his calculations were correct, out into the hall and down the stairs before he landed in the couch cushions he had placed at the bottom of the stairs. Unfortunately for Timmy, he wasn't very good at math and his calculations were rarely correct. As he pushed off the top bunk, Timmy was on a crash course for his bedroom closet.

Timmy wasn't going fifty miles an hour when he hit the bike jump. But he was going fast enough to send him sailing four feet into the air, through his closet doors, and headfirst right through the back wall of his closet.

"What the . . ." he said.

Timmy didn't move. His head was completely embedded in the wall. After several seconds he let out a little cough and shook the dust from his hair. One minute he was traveling headfirst down the ramp, well on his way to becoming the world's greatest stuntman, and the next—the next minute he was launched headfirst into the wall—or a secret room behind it.

Timmy had set out to discover what it must have felt like to be Evel Knievel, flying high over the Snake River Canyon, but instead he had discovered Vincent Shadow's secret attic invention laboratory.

FAME AND FOG

2

Minneapolis, Minnesota

Vincent Shadow used two rolls of duct tape to connect nine garden hoses that he had borrowed from his neighbors. The garden hoses stretched from the kitchen through the living room, up the stairs, in and out of his stepsisters' bedrooms, into the bathroom (where it ran in and out of a bathtub full of ice), and all the way back downstairs to the kitchen. A two-hundred-foot journey in all. A journey made possible by the generosity of Vincent Shadow's new neighbors.

As much as Vincent hated all the attention he had received for winning the annual Whizzer Toys invention contest, it had definitely made building his inventions easier. When he went door-to-door asking to borrow his neighbors' garden hoses, they were all eager to help the now-famous young inventor.

"Whatcha working on now, Vincent? A water hose that plays music? I betcha got a lot of ideas in that head of yours, don't cha," Mr. Johnston said.

"Ah, yeah. I guess so," Vincent replied.

But the truth was that Vincent had nothing. He hadn't had an idea hit him since he and his family moved to Minnesota five months ago. And to make matters worse, summer vacation was just two weeks away, which meant that his summer internship at Whizzer Toys was just two weeks away. Vincent would be spending his summer with the great toy inventor Howard G. Whiz himself. Howard was sure to expect inventions like Vincent's windless kite or his winning Pop Tunz sound bubbles. But, in a fit of frustration with all of his mishaps, Vincent had left all his inventions and notebooks in his secret attic lab back in New York. Now he had nothing. No notebooks. No new toys. No blinding inspiration. Nothing.

In an attempt to remedy this situation, Vincent purchased a shiny new black Moleskine notebook shortly after moving to Minnesota. He sat down and tried to fill it with all the inventions he could remember. But he only remembered a dozen or so. And most of them didn't work. Sky Writerz was one of those inventions. And now he was desperate to make it work.

Sky Writerz was a toy that would allow people to draw or write in midair with colored fog. Or at least Vincent had hoped it would. He had built several prototypes back in New York, but he was never able to make them work. The fog always drifted upward and the art ended up looking like something his mom would have liked: A Jackson Pollock painting, albeit a floating Jackson Pollock painting. But watching his breath hang in the cold Minnesota air had given him an idea. Maybe if he cooled the fog it would remain dense and hang in the air, like his breath on cold Minnesota mornings.

He dumped a gallon of water and two bottles of his sister's hand lotion into the fog machine. He needed glycerin to make fog and the label on his sister's fancy lotion claimed it was ninety-nine percent pure glycerin. Vincent lowered his safety goggles over his eyes and pushed the on button. The fog machine sat quietly. Then it hissed and a small amount of smoke escaped from the duct-taped hoses. It smelled like lilacs, but Vincent didn't notice. He was too excited about the possibility of being the first person to create art in midair. Not even Picasso could make that claim.

Just then the hose began to shake violently. Vincent heard a loud crash upstairs. He set the end of the hose down and ran up the stairs to investigate. He had experienced dozens of mishaps in his old lab: cuts, scrapes, and explosions were just part of the job. In fact, it was the rare experiment that didn't have some sort of mishap. So Vincent was prepared for the worst when he walked into the bathroom. But he found nothing. The hose was still coiled under several pounds of ice. He checked all three of his stepsisters' bedrooms. Nothing. Nothing had exploded, imploded, or combusted.

"I must be getting—"

"VINCENT SHADOW!"

Vincent's self-congratulatory thoughts were interrupted by his stepsister Stella's scream.

"VINCENT, WHERE ARE YOU? WHAT'S GOING ON?" Stella yelled.

Vincent ran out of a bedroom and into a thick blanket of fog. He couldn't see a thing.

"I'm upstairs," he yelled.

"What's going on?" Stella demanded.

"Ah, looks like another failed experiment. Unfortunately," Vincent said, sounding defeated.

"You'd better get down here and get rid of this— this colored fog. Mom is gonna be home any minute.

And"—Stella waved her hand in front of her face—"what is that? It smells like—VINCENT SHADOW, DID YOU USE MY NEW LOTION?"

"All in the name of science, Sis. All in the name of science."

Vincent sat down and decided to wait for the fog, and his sister, to settle down.

PACKAGE FROM HOWARD

3

"Good grief! It's freezing in here! Why are the windows open? And why are these fans on?" Vincent's stepmom Vibs demanded.

Vincent looked at Stella.

"Ah . . . well. It's May, Mom," Stella said.

"Yes. May in Minnesota." Vibs closed the living room windows and turned off the fans. "But I must admit, you can smell spring in the air. It smells like lilacs."

"Where's my dad?" Vincent asked.

"Oh, will you go help him, Vincent? There's a huge package on the front step."

"Huge package?"

Vincent opened the front door and was knocked to the floor by a giant box.

"Oh. Hey, sorry, buddy. I didn't see you there. This thing weighs a ton!" Vincent's dad, Norton Shadow, slid the six-foot-long box into the living room.

"I'm okay. What's in this thing? Who's it from?"

"Looks like it's from Whizzer Toys."

"Come on. Open it, Vincent," said Stella.

"It's huge." Vincent ripped the flaps off the top of the box and peered inside. "Cool!"

"What is it?" Stella tried to peek in the box.

"It's full of toys!" Vincent pulled out a box of classic Whizzer Windupz.

"Now that takes me back. I had those when I was your age." Vincent's dad took the box from Vincent's hand. "Man, I loved my Whizzer Windupz. Look at these, honey!"

"Great. We don't have room for all this stuff," Vibs said.

Vincent pulled out a lime-green Whizzer Wall Racerz, a box of Balloon-E-Toonz, four bottles of Whizzer Sno-Glowz, and—

"Whoa, a new Whizzer Board 4000!" The box tipped over as Vincent pulled out the chromed inline skateboard. "Awesome!"

Vincent's other stepsisters, Anna and Gwen, walked

through the door just as Vincent pushed down on the Whizzer board's turbo pedal. The wheels spun.

"No fair! Why does Vincent get new toys?" Anna demanded.

"They're from Whizzer Toys," Norton replied. "It must all be part of winning the contest."

"No fair. Vincent gets everything!" Anna shouted.

Ignoring her, Vincent leaned the Whizzer Board against the wall and climbed back into the box.

"There's an Air It Out Golf Tee, My Surprise Garden, a whole bunch of Whizzer Bubble Capz, a Fairy Featherz doll, a—"

"VINCENT!" Vibs noticed that she was yelling and lowered her voice. "Vincent. Maybe you could at least give the Fairy Featherz doll to Anna? It's a girl toy, and they're her favorite."

"Sure." Vincent agreed, handing it to Anna.

Anna took the doll and ran up the stairs.

"What else is there?" Stella asked.

"Just some sort of old wooden crate. And it's heavy. Can you give me a hand with it?"

Stella helped Vincent slide the wooden crate from the box onto the floor. It was covered with dirt and scrapes and secured with a large metal lock.

"Where's the key?" Stella asked.

"I don't know." Vincent fumbled through the stack of toys. "I didn't see one."

Stella shook the cardboard box. "That's so weird."

"Hey, can you help me get this stuff downstairs before Anna decides she wants all of it?"

NOT-SO-SECRET LAB

4

Vincent's basement bedroom wasn't really a bedroom at all. It was more like a small closet in the laundry room. But he'd made the best of it. He'd taken over a small workbench in the corner and planned to convert most of the laundry room into his new invention lab. He was thankful that he no longer needed to hide his lab or his inventing. But Stella was still the only one who knew about the source of Vincent's inventions—his blinding headaches that he dismissed as migraines to the rest of the family.

"Careful," Vincent said as he and Stella carried the crate down the basement stairs.

"Sorry. This thing's heavy," Stella said. "What do you think it is?"

"I don't know. Maybe a bunch of old Whizzer toys," Vincent said.

"Yeah, the cast-iron kind," Stella said. "Or maybe it's research. Maybe it's full of old Wondrous Whizzer Wishbooks."

"Yeah. That'd be cool. Let's put it up on the workbench next to Nikola's cage." Vincent and Stella slowly lifted the crate up onto the workbench and set it next to his pet parrot, Nikola. Vincent slid an anvil under the lock and grabbed a hammer.

"What're you doing?" Stella asked as she grabbed his hand.

"I'm gonna see what's inside this old thing."

"But what if—"

SMACK! A spark jumped as Vincent struck the lock. "Nothing," he said.

SMACK!

SMACK!

SMACK!

Stella shielded her eyes.

"Not even a scratch," Vincent said as he examined the lock. "I suppose I could cut the crate open."

"What if you wreck whatever is inside? Or what if Mr. Whiz wants the crate back?"

"We could cut the lock with a blowtorch," Vincent suggested. He had always wanted to use a blowtorch.

"Yeah, and burn the house down. No way. Besides, where are you going to get a blowtorch? Let's go look for a key one more time," Stella said. "Maybe it fell when you were pulling the toys out of the box. It seems weird for Mr. Whiz not to have included a key."

"Or a letter," Vincent added.

Stella said, "Well, at least you got a box of cool toys."

"Yeah. I can't wait to tell the guys at school tomorrow that I finally got a Whizzer Board."

LOBSTER TELEPHONE

5

Vincent, Stella, Gwen, and Anna all attended the Minneapolis School of Art and Design, which was attached to the Minneapolis Institute of Art, a world-class museum—and the place where Norton worked. The students at MSAD took classes like math, science, and English. But most of the classes focused on the arts. Vincent loved art. And he particularly loved his Art Ideas class taught by Mr. Dennis.

"So cool. Dude, I wish I had a Whizzer Board," Vincent's friend Gary said as they waited for Mr. Dennis.

"What else did you get, Vincent?" John asked.

"Ah, there was a big box of Bubble Capz, a Color Doodlez, and an Air It Out Golf Tee."

"Aw, dude. You're so lucky."

"Yeah, but most of that stuff is pretty old," John said. "I mean it's cool and everything, but I've got most of that stuff already."

"Ahhh. There he is," Mr. Dennis said as he dragged two large garbage bags into the classroom, "the winner of this year's Whizzer Toys contest! Welcome home, Mr. Shadow! Welcome home! Did you have a good week in New York?"

"Yes. Thanks, Mr. D."

"And how is that famous toy-inventing cousin of mine, Mr. Howard G. Whiz, doing?"

"He's good."

"We saw you on the news, Vincent. Those bubbles were spectacular! Just spectacular. But I must ask, what happened to the windless kite?"

"There was an accident the night before the contest."

"Ah. So you were able to invent a new toy . . . overnight? Amazing. Just amazing! See, class, there's always more than one right answer, isn't there, Mr. Shadow?"

"I guess so, Mr. D."

"Speaking of right answers—class, please stand up."

Vincent, Mike, John, Gary, Eleanor, and Lori all stood up.

"Where's Ariel?"

"Well, Mr. D, she, ah, she decided to switch to Mr. Gang's ceramics class," said Gary .

"Right. And then there were six. Well, come on, class, we don't have all day."

"Where are we going, Mr. D?" Gary asked.

"To find some answers, my dear Gary. To find some answers."

Gary looked at the sculpture and laughed. He couldn't help it.

"It's a telephone shaped like a lobster, Mr. D."

"Yes, indeed it is, Gary. Salvador Dalí created the Lobster Telephone in 1936. Brilliant, isn't it?"

"I guess so, Mr. D. But wouldn't it, like, pinch your ear off if you tried to use it?"

"Well, yes. If it were alive, I believe it would."

"This is pretty wild," John said, pointing to Salvador Dalí's Les Chimeres.

"What is it?" Eleanor asked.

"Oh, it looks like this line is a dude holding a flashlight or maybe a hose. And this, this squiggly thing kind of makes the front of a truck," John said. "Maybe he's a fireman putting out a fire."

"Truck? Where's the truck? I don't see a fire truck. I see this guy," Eleanor said, pointing to a heavy black line. "Fishing in this pond."

"Pond? That's no pond. This here," Gary said as he pointed to two circles near the bottom of the canvas, "this bull is charging this group of people."

"Group of people? Those are just dots," John said.

"I got it. It's like, the running-with-the-bulls thing. Isn't it, Mr. D?" Gary asked.

"Yes," Mr. Dennis answered.

"Ha! See? I knew it. I'm good at this art stuff," Gary said.

"Yes, Gary, you are good at this art stuff. It is also a fireman putting out a fire and someone fishing."

"What?" Gary said, now sounding defeated.

"Class, who has heard the expression 'Art is in the eye of the beholder?'"

Eleanor raised her hand. "It means we all see art differently?"

"Right, Ms. Eleanor. We all see art differently. Mr. Dalí believed that we all see art—and the world—differently. Mr. Dalí was part of a group of artists who practiced something called 'surrealism.' Surrealist artists would often look for connections between things that seem unrelated."

"Oh, like how John says he is related to Ben Franklin, but no one believes him?"

"Well, Lori, more like splattering paint on a canvas and seeing how it starts to form a person or a pond or—"

"Or a bull," Gary added.

"Right. Or a bull."

"That seems like a weird way to make art, doesn't it, Mr. D?" Gary asked.

"Well, let's find out. I'd like all of you to try this at home. Take some seemingly unrelated items and connect them in some new way. It can be splashes of paint, items found outside, or things lying around your house. Just put them together in a new and exciting way! This is the last assignment of the year, so let's make it great."

ICE SPOON

6

Vincent placed his face inches away from
the plate and tried to flip some corn into his mouth. He
missed and several kernels landed in Gwen's hair. She
didn't notice. But Anna did.

"Vincent flicked corn in Gwen's hair!"

Gwen rocked back and forth in her chair. She was
clueless. She had headphones in her ears and corn in
her bangs.

"Sorry," Vincent said. "Accident. Oh, Stella, tell everyone about your award."

"An award?" Vibs asked. "What for, honey?"

"Nothing, really. Just a little thing I did at school," Stella said, trying to dismiss the question.

"Little? There's nothing little about it," Vincent said. "At assembly this morning, Mrs. Schmidt gave Stella an award for outstanding achievement in fiction."

"Seven other people got one too," Stella added.

"That's great, honey," Vibs said. "What did you write?"

"It was a story called *The Last Magic Show* about this old magician who vanishes during his last performance."

"Fantastic. I would love to—" Norton was interrupted.

"HEY!" Gwen yelled as several pieces of corn pelted her in the eye.

"Sorry," Vincent said. He pushed his spoon around the plate in an effort to get something, anything, into his mouth.

"What *are* you doing?" Vibs demanded.

Vincent's sleeve was dripping wet as he held up what was left of his ice spoon.

"I'm trying to eat?"

"With what? What is that?"

"I call it the Ice Spoon. It's homework."

"Homework? Let me guess. Homework for Mr. Dennis?" Vibs asked.

"Yup," Vincent replied, sucking on what was left of his spoon. "We're supposed to put two unrelated

things together and make something new." The last piece of spoon melted between his fingers.

"And you put a spoon together . . . with ice?" Vibs asked.

"Yup."

"That's dumb. You're gonna get an F," Anna said, smiling.

"Yup," Vincent agreed.

MY HOMEWORK MELTED

7

"Incredible, Lori. Just incredible. And it really works?" Mr. Dennis asked.

"Oh yeah. We can go outside and I'll show you. 'Course we'll have to wait for the snow to come back, but—"

"No, I believe you. Fantastic! Who wants to go next?"

"Oh, me! Me! Me! Mr. D!"

"Okay, Gary. What wonderful things did you put together?"

Gary reached under his desk and pulled out a large hockey glove covered in duct tape.

"It's a fork!" Gary announced proudly.

"Well, well, well." Mr. Dennis moved closer and saw the tip of a fork hot-glued to the end of a metal tube that had been duct-taped to the hockey glove. "Well, yes, it is indeed a fork. Tell us about it, Mr. Gary. How did you get the idea for the . . . for this fork glove?"

"Oh no, Mr. D. This isn't a fork glove. This is the Fork-Master 4000. My dad likes to call it the Ultimate Fork." Gary smiled. "You see, Mr. D, I was sitting at the dinner table eating one of my mom's steaks and telling my parents about our homework. You know, the lobster phone and all that stuff. So, I was telling them the story and trying to cut my steak at the same time. But my mom's steaks are real hard to cut. Even for my dad. So my dad, as a joke, got up and grabbed the power saw out of the garage and pretended to cut his steak with it. And that's how I got the idea."

"So it has a saw built into the glove?" John asked.

"No." Gary pushed a button and a red laser beam shot out the end of the fork. He pretended to cut an invisible steak on his desk.

"You see, it gives you a guideline to cut to, just like my dad's saw."

"Ah, well done, you." Mr. Dennis clapped.

"So what's with the glove then?" Lori asked.

"Protection, silly. My dad wouldn't let me use a saw without protection."

"Okay. Very good. Who's next, class? Mr. Shadow? Would you like to share your project?"

Vincent didn't say a word. He desperately wished the blinding spells would return. He needed a good idea. And he needed it fast. How could he follow the Ultimate Fork with the Ice Spoon? Plus, he was pretty sure his new spoon had melted by now.

"I'm still working on mine, Mr. D. Can I show it next week?"

"Yes. Fine. What a great way to end the year. I'm sure it will be brilliant, Mr. Shadow. Just brilliant."

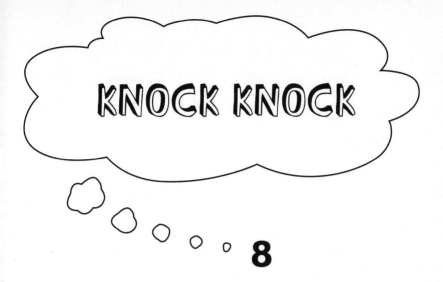

KNOCK KNOCK

8

African gray parrots are considered to be among the most intelligent animals on the planet. They are capable of learning thousands of words. And Vincent's African gray, Nikola, was no exception. Vincent's parents had purchased Nikola for Vincent's ninth birthday. And Vincent quickly went about the business of teaching Nikola to talk. He thought it would be fun to have a pet that told jokes. So he read entire books

KNOCK
KNOCK

of knock-knock jokes to Nikola. Vincent had read hundreds of knock-knock jokes to him, something the entire Shadow family would soon regret. Nikola loved the reaction he received when he told a joke. So he started telling jokes all day. Every day. No one in the Shadow house had laughed at his knock-knock jokes in years. No one but Nikola. He always said, "Ha, ha" after he told a joke.

"Knock knock."

Vincent ignored Nikola. But he knew it wouldn't work. It never worked.

"Knock knock."

"Not now, Nikola."

"Knock knock."

"Fine. Who's there?"

"Who."

"Who who?"

"I'm a parrot, not an owl, silly. Ha, ha," Nikola said.

"What am I going to do, Nikola? I need to get my project done. It's due tomorrow and I've got nothing." Vincent had tried all week to put two seemingly unconnected things together. But he had been unsuccessful. He lay down on his bed, desperately hoping for a flash of inspiration. Or something. Anything.

"Knock knock."

Vincent put a pillow over his head.

Vincent's first toy idea had hit him on his eighth birthday. And ideas continued to hit him on a fairly regular basis after that. Until his family moved to Minnesota. Then they stopped. And, for the most part, Vincent welcomed the break. When inventions came to Vincent, they hit him hard. They hit him so hard that the invention was the only thing Vincent could see. The toy inventions would float in front of his eyes. Whole and complete. Vincent could spin the toys in any direction and see every detail. But the toys were all he could see. They would blind him to the world around him. Sometimes for a few minutes. Sometimes for hours. Vincent hid his unusual talent from the world by claiming to have "blinding headaches."

The blind spells were always inconvenient. But sometimes they were downright dangerous—like the time Vincent had the idea for Sketch FX Markerz as he and his mother were riding their bikes through Central Park. But one time an idea came to Vincent at just the right moment. He smiled at the memory. It was the night of his ninth birthday. The night his parents gave him his parrot.

Dylan Thomas had been Vincent's best friend growing up. The two always had sleepovers for each other's birthday. For Vincent's ninth birthday his parents decided to take the boys to a haunted house being put on by the cast and crew of *The Phantom of the Opera*.

"What could be better than real actors putting on a haunted house? This will be fun," Vincent's mom said as they stood in line.

And she was right. The haunted house was good. Maybe too good. Vincent was shaking as he, Dylan, and his mom and dad grabbed onto a rope and were led through a black curtain. Vincent remembered seeing a woman with real snakes in her hair. Then the room went dark and bright lights quickly moved toward him. The lights grew brighter as they approached. He heard a deep growl. The pair of lights were now the only thing Vincent could see. They were floating just inches from his face. Vincent heard screams in the distance. And then his mom screamed. Then his dad.

"Did you see that?" Dylan asked. "I think it was a real bat."

"Bat?" Vincent said.

Vincent's mom and dad both screamed again. Vincent didn't see a bat. In fact, Vincent realized he couldn't see anything but these—"Headlights," he said out loud.

"Yeah, turn on the lights!" his dad screamed.

Vincent was spinning the idea around in his head. It was idea number sixteen. He would call it "Pump-Up Pickup." It was a toy truck with working headlights and a built-in pump that inflated the tires, transforming the small truck into a monster truck.

"OH NO!" Dylan yelled. "IS THAT A CHAIN SAW?"

For the next twenty minutes Vincent relaxed and enjoyed his newest toy invention while Dylan and his parents continued to scream, enduring what his dad would later refer to as "the scariest twenty minutes of my life." Dylan went on to have nightmares for the next six months. And, unfortunately, due to what Dylan's parents called "poor parental judgment," Dylan was never allowed to sleep over at Vincent's house again.

"Knock knock."

Vincent pulled the pillow from his head.

"That's it!"

"Eye patch," Nikola said.

"I can use the Pump-Up Pickup for my homework!"

"Eye patch ya like this joke. Ha! Ha!"

Vincent set a Tonka truck on his workbench, then yelled up the stairs, "Stellllllllaaaa!"

Stella stuck her head down the steps. "What's up?"

"I need to build my project for Mr. Dennis. Can you help me move the Whizzer crate out of the way?"

"Whatcha gonna build?" Stella asked as they each grabbed a side of the crate.

"A monster truck," Vincent replied. "On three. One, two, three."

They lifted the old wooden crate with ease.

"That's weird," Stella said.

"Yeah. How did the crate get lighter?"

"What in the world did Mr. Whiz send you?" Stella asked.

WIZARD OF THE UPPER WEST SIDE

9

Vincent walked into the kitchen where his dad and Vibs were eating breakfast. It was 6:46 AM. He hadn't slept. Between building the Pump-Up Pickup and being nervous about his summer internship, he couldn't sleep.

"You're up early this morning," Vibs said. "Excited about the last day of school?"

"I guess so."

"So, what's that? The latest invention by the great Vincent Shadow?" Norton asked, pointing to the truck in Vincent's hand as he choked down a piece of peanut butter and buttered toast.

"No, just my assignment for Mr. D's class," Vincent said. He set the Pump-Up Pickup on the kitchen table.

"What happened to the Ice Spoon?"

"Anna was right. It wasn't very good," Vincent said.

"Hey, is that my bike pump?" Norton asked.

"Yeah. I'm using it to inflate the truck's tires. Is that okay? I'll give it back when I'm done."

"Sure, I guess," Norton said. "Oh, hey, I talked to Aunt Bonnie last night and everything is set for Sunday. She'll pick you up at the airport."

"I still don't know about this, Norton," Vibs said. "Vincent is pretty young to be flying to New York all by himself."

Vincent didn't say anything. He half agreed with Vibs. He almost hoped Vibs would forbid him to go.

"Nonsense, honey. He'll be fine. I'll take him all the way to the gate and talk to the flight attendants myself."

"Aunt Bonnie isn't so young any more, Norton. Do you really think that—"

"Trust me. Aunt Bonnie is gonna outlive all of us."

"What is he doing on TV?" Stella asked as she walked into the kitchen.

Vincent looked up at the television.

"What the—"

"Quick, turn it up!" Stella shouted.

"Thanks, Cindy," the TV reporter said, looking directly into the camera. "I'm Kent Bloomingtrip and I'm standing here outside the Spinowski Toy Company. Joining me is the head of Spinowski Toys, George Spinowski. And this amazing young toy inventor is Timmy Zimmerman." The reporter put his arm around Timmy. "Better

known to his friends and
family as Danger Boy."

Stella looked at Vincent.
"Toy inventor?"

"Well, I call him a genius,"
George Spinowski said
as he leaned toward the
microphone.

"Young Timmy has invented not one, not two, but
dozens of toys that, well"— the reporter laughed—
"you truly have to see to believe. Timmy, can you show
our viewers some of your inventions?"

"Sure." Timmy put on a diver's mask and placed a
snorkel in his mouth. "I call this one Sonic Snorkelz."

"What?" said the reporter.

"Sonic Snorkelz!" Timmy yelled into the
mouthpiece.

"Snakey Quarkels?" the reporter asked.

Timmy removed the snorkel.

"No, Sonic Snorkelz. I call this Sonic Snorkelz. Maybe you have to be underwater for it to work," Timmy said.

"That little weasel!" Stella shouted.

". . . And I call this the Rockitez." Timmy jumped on the Rockitez launch pad—a launch pad Vincent and his mother had built. The cameraman tried to follow the Rockitez as it soared high into the sky and popped into a kite.

"Wow, that's truly amazing," Norton said out loud.

The reporter bent down and picked up Vincent's Sketch N' Sculpt Markerz. "Here, show the folks this toy," the reporter said, looking back into the camera. "You're going to love this."

Timmy shook the marker, removed the cap, and began to draw.

"Don't shake it!" Vincent yelled at the TV.

Timmy drew a picture of a motorcycle. The tires appeared to magically inflate as the ink grew off the page.

"Amazing!" the reporter exclaimed. "And that's not even the half of it. There are a dozen more. Each one more amazing then the next, right?"

George Spinowski leaned toward the microphone again. "Yes. He just walked into our office last week with notebooks filled with toy ideas!"

"Notebooks-ful? Wow. You're truly an inspiration. Where do you get your ideas, Timmy?"

"Yeah, Timmy. Tell everyone where you get your ideas." Stella was now inches from the TV. Vincent sat motionless.

"Move, Stella," Vibs said. "I can't see."

"Well, I don't know. I guess I just—just kind of find them around."

"And this is your mother?" the reporter asked.

"Yup."

"Well, Mrs. Zimmerman. You must be very proud of your son."

"Oh, I am."

"When did you first realize your son was a genius?"

"Genius? Wow. I don't know. I guess Timmy has always been different—you know? Always getting into one thing or another," Mrs. Zimmerman said.

"Right. And now Mr. Spinowski. Spinowski Toys has purchased all of Timmy's amazing inventions. Is that right?"

"That is correct."

"Like this amazing football that bites your hand when you try to catch it." The reporter put his hand in the mouth of the Biting Beast Ball.

"Yes, we call that one the Super Monster Football. You just pull the tongue—" Spinowski pulled on the Beast Ball's tongue and its mouth opened. "And then throw it like a regular football. It will bite down on your friend's arm. We hope to have it in stores in the next few months."

"Super Monster Football?" Stella asked out loud.

"Sshh," Vibs said.

"Well, it looks like you've got your work cut out for you with all of these inventions," the reporter said.

"Yes we do. Keeping up with this, this little wizard will be a challenge," Spinowski said, patting Timmy on the shoulder. "But we at Spinowski Toys are up for the challenge. We've been making amazing products here since 1935."

"There you have it, folks." The reporter stepped closer to the camera. "I'm sure we're going to be seeing lots more of young Timmy. This is Kent Bloomingtrip reporting live with the young wizard of the Upper West Side."

"That fraud!" Stella jumped up. "That little fraud!"

Vincent didn't move.

"Vincent, you have to say something!" Stella said as she pulled on Vincent's arm.

"Stella! Calm down," Vibs said. "It is okay to have more than one young toy inventor on TV."

"She's right. His inventions are great, Vincent," said Norton. "I mean, that pen—wow! But you know that doesn't take away from anything you've done, right?"

"No, Mom. It's not right!" Stella yelled.

Vincent didn't say a word.

"Come on, champ, I mean, look at this truck," Norton picked up Vincent's latest creation. It had balloons for tires and a bicycle pump duct-taped to the back.

"This is great too." Norton pushed down on the pump and all four tires exploded.

"Oh, no! I'm sorry, buddy. I'm sure we can fix it."

Vincent got up and put the milk carton back in the refrigerator. He had lost his appetite. First Danger Boy stole his inventions and now his final assignment of the year for Mr. Dennis had exploded. A drawing caught Vincent's eye as he closed the refrigerator door. He pulled the drawing from the door. There, under flow-

ers and hearts drawn in crayon and red permanent marker, lay a familiar shape. It was the Tesla device he had seen in Mr. Whiz's Room of Firsts. The vacuum tube Tesla coil.

"What's this?"

"Oh, those are Anna's collages. Aren't they neat?" Vibs answered.

Vincent looked back at the refrigerator door. There, covered in pink crayon and red marker, were dozens of Tesla's invention sketches.

"Hey, champ. Don't forget to take your migraine medicine this morning," Vincent's dad said.

LOST AND FOUND

10

BANG! BANG! BANG!

"Anna, I know you're in there!" Vincent said, pounding on the bathroom door.

BANG! BANG! BANG!

"Open the door, Anna. NOW!"

"Go away!"

"NOW, ANNA!"

Anna flung the door open and pushed her way past Vincent.

"There! You can have it!" Anna said as she ran into her room and tried to slam the door. Vincent stuck his foot in the doorway and shoved a fistful of Tesla sketches through the opening.

"Explain this!" Vincent demanded.

Anna tried to grab the sketches. "Hey, those are mine."

"Where did you get these?" Vincent pushed the door open.

"Get out!" Anna cried.

Vincent couldn't believe his eyes. Anna's walls were covered with the Tesla sketches. Highly detailed, scientific pencil sketches covered with daisies, kitties, and pink bunnies.

Above Anna's bed was a sketch of a Tesla turbine.

The rotor was barely visible behind the spotted puppy Anna had painted over it. And Tesla's direct beam particle charger was hanging over Anna's desk with a picture of two little guinea pigs jumping rope pasted on top of it.

Suddenly, it all made sense to Vincent.

"Where is it?" Vincent asked as he started pulling the sketches off the wall.

"Where's what?"

"The key. Where's the key?"

Stella heard the commotion and walked into the room. "What's all of this?"

"There is no mysterious invention making the crate lighter. It's Anna. Somehow she's going into the crate and taking these." Vincent showed Stella one of the Tesla sketches. "She must have found a key."

"Give it back, Anna," Stella said.

"It's mine! I found it stuck to—"

"Give it back NOW!" Stella demanded.

Anna reached in her pocket, pulled out a black metal key, and handed it to Stella.

LITTLE PINK BUNNIES

11

"**What's under the towel?**" the flight attendant asked.

"My pet parrot, Nikola. I covered his cage so he wouldn't talk," Vincent replied.

"Wow, he talks?"

"Oh, yeah. He talks a lot."

The flight attendant handed Vincent a bag of peanuts.

"Those are nice drawings." She motioned to Anna's art stacked on the tray in front of him. "Cute bunnies."

"Oh, they're not mine. My obnoxious little sister did those."

"I see," she said as she handed Vincent a Coke. "I had one of those too—obnoxious little sisters, that is." The flight attendant smiled. "My name is Kisha. Let me know if you need anything."

"Thanks," said Vincent.

Vincent pulled the letter from his pocket and read it for the hundredth time that day.

Dearest Vincent,

Congratulations again on winning this year's Whizzer Toys contest!

It is with great anticipation and joy that I await your arrival. I truly believe that greater forces have conspired to bring you into my life at this most critical time, for a talent and mind such as yours is truly a rare and special occurrence. I have spent much of my life fostering young inventors and encouraging them to follow their dreams. But, alas, it is I who must ask a favor of you.

I, like you, have long admired the incredible life and work of Nikola Tesla. The gifts Tesla bestowed unto us are countless. Not a day passes when we do not all benefit from the fruits of his labor. Yet, due to the extraordinary claims he made at the end of his life, Tesla died penniless and an object of ridicule. I intend to correct this inexcusable injustice. But I can't do it without you, Vincent. I believe you may be the only person who can help unravel Tesla's secrets and right this terrible wrong.

Tesla had been working on some extraordinary inventions at the end of his life. And he claimed to have working prototypes. Now, I have those prototypes. As well as all of Tesla's notes and sketches from the last years of his life. I believe I'm close to making Tesla's greatest dream a reality, but I fear I don't have the time, or strength, to see it through. I believe, however, that you do. I could see it in your kite invention. In your bubble invention. And in your eyes.

I have enclosed all of Tesla's notebooks for your review. Vincent, Tesla's secret lies within these

pages! I look forward to your thoughts and spend-
ing the summer together. Good-bye for now.

Sincerely,
Howard G. Whiz

Vincent set the letter down and leaned back in his seat. He looked at the stack of sketches Anna had ripped out of Tesla's notebooks. Tesla's greatest secrets were now covered in bunnies, puppies, and kitties.

TIME IN A BOTTLE

12

Some of the most important inventions in history were unveiled at the 1939 New York World's Fair. The television, microwave, copy machine, dishwasher, jet engine, computer, robot, and fluorescent light, as well as nylon, Plexiglas, and 3D movies were all unveiled there. But perhaps the most popular exhibit at the fair was Westinghouse's Time Capsule.

Scientists at Westinghouse developed an eight-hundred-pound time capsule made out of a special alloy capable of resisting the effects of time for five thousand years. Carefully selected items were placed inside the time capsule and the capsule was buried fifty feet below the fairground in New York's Flushing

Meadows Park. There it would remain sealed until the year 6939 AD.

The Time Capsule's carefully selected items included a note from Albert Einstein, various fabrics, metals, plastics, and seeds, a Sears, Roebuck catalog, a dictionary, an alarm clock, a baseball, eyeglasses, a toothbrush, a print of *The Persistence of Memory* by Salvador Dalí, the instructions to the game pinball, invented by the young Howard G. Whiz—and several of Nikola Tesla's invention notebooks.

Nikola Tesla had gained worldwide fame forty-six years earlier when he and Westinghouse provided electricity to the great Chicago World's Fair of 1893. More than half the country made their way to the Chicago World's Fair to see the electric light. Over the next forty-six years Tesla would continue to wow the world with inventions like the radio, remote control, X-ray machines, neon lights, and radar.

On September 23, 1938 a variety of scientists, inventors, and politicians gathered for the ceremonial burying of the Time Capsule. And young Howard G. Whiz could not believe his luck when he found himself standing next to the great Nikola Tesla. Howard was mesmerized by the eccentric inventor. Tesla spoke to the young boy and told Howard stories about what he thought the world might look like when the time capsule was opened. The two inventors, at opposite ends of life, discussed science, inventing, and the future. Howard was so impressed by Tesla that he was sure he would remember every word of their conversation for the rest of his life. And he did. Even now, at almost eighty-one years old, Howard could hear Tesla's voice say:

"I do not think there is any thrill that can go through the human heart like that of an inventor as he sees some creation of the brain unfolding to success."

Howard hung on Tesla's every word and spent the rest of his life following in Tesla's footsteps. Young Howard G. Whiz went on to create the Whizzer Toy Company and invent some of the most beloved toys in history.

But as important as Tesla was to the world, he died penniless and alone just four years after Howard first met him. In the final years of his life Tesla made claims to wild inventions: inventions like earthquake machines, death ray devices, thought recorders, and wireless power. And although he claimed to have working prototypes, and proof of these inventions, the world turned its back on him. No one believed in the eccentric old inventor. No one except Howard G. Whiz.

And so, finally, after a lifetime of success with toy inventing, Howard turned his focus back to Tesla. He was determined to show the world it had been wrong to doubt Nikola Tesla's brilliant claims. Howard spent twelve years—and much of his fortune—collecting all the Tesla artifacts he could find. And he put together the largest collection in the world. It included many of Tesla's most secret prototypes and notebooks from the last years of his life. But as hard as Howard tried, he was unable to solve the mysteries surrounding some of Tesla's greatest inventions. And as Howard's health declined, he feared that Tesla's greatest secrets would remain secrets forever. He spent many sleepless nights in his lab, poring over Tesla's notes, looking and hoping for a clue. A miracle. As Howard packed the last of Tesla's notebooks into the old wooden crate, he was sure he had found his miracle in young Vincent Shadow.

ITTY BITTY AUNT BONNIE

13

"What's your aunt's name?" Kisha asked
Vincent as they stood waiting on the airport sidewalk.

"Bonnie," Vincent replied.

"And you're sure she knew what time your flight was coming in?"

"Yeah, I'm sure...I think," Vincent said. "You can't miss her. She drives the biggest car you've ever seen."

"Vinny!" she yelled.

"Aunt Bonnie?" Vincent walked around to the driver's side of the ITTY.

"Oh, honey. It's so good to see you back in New York," Aunt Bonnie said as she hugged Vincent.

"It's good to be home," said Vincent.

"Okay, Vincent," Kisha said. "I'd better get back to work. Don't forget Nikola," she added as she handed Vincent the covered cage.

"Thanks."

"Oh, you brought your bird?" Aunt Bonnie asked.

"Yeah. I hope you don't mind. I just thought he would be lonely with me gone all summer."

"Oh, hon. No problem. I'm sure we'll all have fun together."

"What happened to the orange car?" Vincent asked.

"I've gone green! And this is a breeze to park."

Vincent stuffed his backpack into the tiny trunk and tried to squeeze his suitcase behind the seat.

"Sorry. There isn't much room. Try pulling your seat all the way forward."

Vincent slid the seat forward and forced his suitcase into the rear of the car. He squeezed into the seat, buckled his seat belt, and tried to pull Nikola's cage onto his lap.

"Pull it hard, Vinny."

Vincent pulled hard. The metal cage bent as he forced it in between him and the ITTY dashboard. Vincent didn't notice that the cage door had popped open.

"It's so good to see you," Bonnie said. "How's your dad? Oh boy, we all miss him so much at the museum. It's just not the same without him. No, not the same at all. You know, they hired this Mr. Jilliver to run the museum after your dad left. And I don't think he would have enjoyed working for Mr. Jilliver. Nope. No sir. No one does. It's just not the same."

"My dad's doing good, I guess." Vincent said. He could hardly breathe. Nikola's cage was jammed into his ribs. Bonnie pulled away from the curb. Every crack in the road felt like a crater in the ITTY. Vincent winced in pain.

"Like just the other day, we got in a new exhibit in and I understand it wasn't the greatest exhibit in the history of the museum, but still, Mr. Jilliver didn't send out any cards. Or put up posters. Or anything. He didn't want to spend the money. So no one came! Not a one! I sat there waiting to take tickets and no one showed. It was so sad. That wouldn't happen when Mr. Velocette and your dad were running the museum."

Vincent groaned. He was sure the cage had poked right into him. Was he bleeding? He could feel something. He looked down. The towel covering the cage was moving.

"Oh, no!" Vincent yelled as a flurry of feathers flew into his face.

Aunt Bonnie screamed. And Nikola screeched as he tried to gain flight. But there was nowhere to fly. Nikola smacked headfirst into the windshield and fell into Aunt Bonnie's lap. Aunt Bonnie screamed again. Nikola used his beak to climb Aunt Bonnie. He climbed up the front of her shirt, pulled himself up onto her shoulders, hopped to her hat, spun around, fluffed his feathers, and nestled in.

"Sorry," Vincent said.

Vincent hoped this wasn't a sign of things to come.

MOSTLY CLOUDY

14

Vincent's entire body was shaking. He opened one eye. Aunt Bonnie was standing directly above him, shaking his shoulder.

"Oh, good morning. Boy, you must have been tired. You were sound asleep. I wish I could sleep like that. Wow! Well, I would've let you sleep in longer, but you don't want to be late on your first day. No sir." Aunt Bonnie turned on the bedroom light.

Vincent looked at the clock. It was 4:55 AM.

"Thanks," Vincent said.

"I'll make you some cereal, hon. I just need to mix up some milk," Aunt Bonnie

said as she walked out of the room.

"Great," Vincent said. *Great*, Vincent thought. He'd forgotten all about Aunt Bonnie's powdered milk.

Vincent rubbed his eyes and followed Aunt Bonnie to the kitchen. He sat down at the kitchen table and watched Aunt Bonnie pull the dusty can from the cupboard. He was sure it had been there since his mother was a little girl.

"So, are you excited for your first day at the toy company?" Bonnie asked as she poured some powder into a pitcher of water.

"I guess so." Vincent's stomach hurt. He wasn't sure if he was worried about telling Howard Whiz that the Tesla sketches were ruined, or just worried about having to drink the cloudy water that Aunt Bonnie was pouring into his glass.

"Are you nervous, Vinny?"

"I guess so," Vincent said, watching the clumps of powder as they settled to the bottom of the glass.

"Oh, don't be nervous. You're going to be great. Just great." She placed the pitcher of milky water into the refrigerator. "Oh, hon, you'd better hurry up and eat. I'll drop you off on my way to the museum. I like to be there by five thirty. I put the coffee on, ya know."

Vincent looked down at the bowl.

"That's strange," he said. Vincent could swear that Cheerios usually floated in milk.

Vincent squeezed out of the ITTY.

"Okay, honey. You have a great day. I'm just across the street. Oh, well, you know that. Goodness. It's not like you didn't grow up here. Well, have a great time and just walk over to the museum when you're done. Good luck, hon. Have fun!" Vincent could hear Aunt Bonnie yelling, "YOU'LL BE GREAT" as she zipped up the street.

Howard G. Whiz lived and worked out of a six-story Gothic mansion called the Carlisle. It was located on the corner of Fifth Avenue and Seventy-eighth Street. Vincent looked down at his watch. Five thirty two AM. He looked up at the Carlisle. It was dark. He wondered if it was too early to ring the bell. He was sure that Howard would hear the bell if he rang it, but Vincent wasn't sure he wanted him to. What would he say? How would he explain Anna's ruining the Tesla sketches? Ruining any chance Howard had of fulfilling his dream? And Tesla's dream? The pain in his stomach grew stronger.

Vincent decided to go for a walk. He crossed Fifth Avenue to Central Park, just as he had done every day of his life. His previous life. Before Minnesota. He walked down the path past Turtle Pond. He crossed the street and kept walking until he was standing in front of his old house. It hadn't changed. The blinds on his old bedroom window were still missing the three rows that Vincent had used as slides in one of his massive Domino Rally undertakings.

"Vincent? Vincent, is that you?"

Vincent turned around as his former neighbor Mrs. Moody picked up her newspaper and adjusted her robe.

"Hi there, Mrs. Moody."

"Well, what are you doing here? Did your dad move back already? I had a feeling he'd be back."

"No. I'm the only one here. I'm staying with my Aunt Bonnie this summer."

"Oh. Well, how is your dad doing?"

"He's good."

"Good, good." Mrs. Moody walked to the curb. "It's so good to see you. You'll have to come to dinner. We miss you around here."

"I miss it here too," Vincent said, looking up at his old room.

"I'll tell you, it's been a circus here since you moved out. An honest-to-goodness circus. That Timmy Zimmerman has half the New York press corps hanging around the neighborhood. They say he's some sort of genius. I say he's trouble with a capital T." Mrs.

Moody shook her rolled-up newspaper at Vincent's old building.

"Yeah, well . . ." Vincent said. "I'd better get going."

"It was good to see you, Vincent. Stop by again."

"Oh, I'm sure I will," Vincent said as he took one last look up at his old bedroom window.

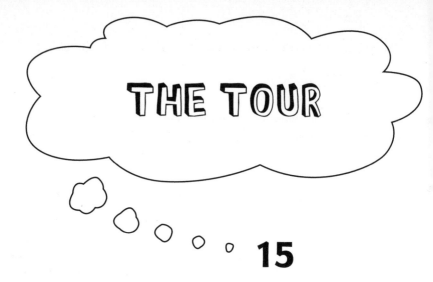

THE TOUR

15

"Hey there! Hey you! Look out!"

Vincent felt something fly inches above his head. He turned around in time to see an object smack into the side of a taxi and land back at his feet.

The cabbie threw his arms up in anger.

"Sorry. Wasn't me," Vincent said.

Vincent bent down and picked up the long black tube. It was shining and heavy and had a white string hanging out of one end. The string was quickly being sucked into the tube.

"Hey!"

Vincent looked around, but didn't see anyone.

"Hey, drop it. Hey! Up here!"

Vincent looked up to see a man hanging out of a second-story window of the Carlisle.

"Hi. Is this—" Vincent started to say.

"THROW IT!" the man yelled.

Vincent looked down just as the last of the string was sucked inside the tube. And then—*KABOOM!*

Vincent threw the tube, but it was too late. It exploded with the force of twenty-five water balloons.

"Yikes! Sorry about that," the man said, disappearing inside the window.

Vincent took his glasses off and wiped them on his shirt. But it was pointless. His shirt was soaked. His pants were soaked. He bounced up and down on his toes; even his shoes had standing water in them.

The front door of the Carlisle flew open and a gray-haired man wearing a Beatles T-shirt ran out.

"Oh, dude! Wow, it really worked. Look at you, you're soaking wet! Cool!"

"Excuse me?" Vincent said.

"Oh, man, I mean, I'm really sorry. I didn't see you there until it was too late. I tried to warn you, though."

"No problem."

"Wow, look at you, though. You gotta admit it was pretty impressive."

"Yeah, I guess so," Vincent replied.

"You've heard of firecrackers, right? I call these Water-crackerz. Just fill them up, pull the string, and run. See, it's the last part you should've known about. The running part."

"Yeah." Vincent was holding his arms straight out at his sides like a scarecrow when Calli Callosum, Howard's longtime personal assistant, came running up the sidewalk.

"Oh, my. Vincent, what happened to you?" Calli asked.

"Vincent?" the man asked. "Oh, no! Dude, you're Vincent Shadow?"

"Yeah."

"Oh, no. I just totally soaked the contest winner," the man said to Calli.

"Oh, Vincent. I'm so sorry. Fayman has a way of getting ahead of himself."

"It's no problem," Vincent said.

"Yeah, sorry again. I'm Fayman," he said, extending his hand to Vincent. "I'm the resident physicist-turned-toy-inventor here. I've been looking forward to meeting you. Howard has said so much about you."

"It's nice to meet you." Vincent shook Fayman's hand.

"Well, come on in and we'll get you dried off," Calli said. "And then I'll give you a tour of this crazy place."

She led the way inside the Carlisle. The lobby was cluttered with boxes and crates.

"Please forgive the mess," Calli said. "Mr. Whiz attended an auction last week and picked up some more memorabilia."

"Yeah, you'll get used to the maze of boxes," Fayman said. "Sometimes I'm not sure if this is a toy company or a museum dedicated to crazy dead inventors."

"FAYMAN!" Calli scolded.

"Okay. Okay. That's my cue. It was nice to meet you, dude. I look forward to working with you."

"You'll have to excuse Fayman. These have been difficult times for all of us." Calli threw her jacket on top of a box. "How much do you know about Whizzer Toys, Vincent?"

"Well, I've been a big fan of Mr. Whiz and his toys my whole life. I use to live just a couple of blocks from here and walked by this building every day. But I had no idea this was the Whizzer Toys building."

"I'm not surprised. Mr. Whiz likes to keep a low profile. Come on, we'll start the tour on the second floor." Calli motioned to the grand staircase in the front lobby. "How old are you, Vincent?"

"Eleven."

"Well, Howard wasn't much older than you when he started Whizzer Toys. He was just eighteen."

"Wow."

"Whizzer Toys has been around for over sixty years. In that time, Whizzer has manufactured over twelve hundred different toys. All of them invented by Howard."

"Twelve hundred?" Vincent was shocked. He had lots of toy ideas, but nowhere near twelve hundred. He had fifty—maybe fifty-five, tops.

"Yes. Howard invents all the toys. But he definitely

has help getting them out. I think you'll find we have a small but amazingly talented group of people here at Whizzer. And I think you'll fit right in." Calli looked back and smiled at Vincent. Vincent wished he shared her confidence.

Calli stopped at the top of the stairs. "This is the main ballroom. We don't eat in here much any more. It's used mostly for special occasions." She continued walking. "The Carlisle has been in Howard's family for two generations. He moved in shortly after his father died. And it has been home to the Whizzer Toy Company ever since. For over forty-three years now. The first floor is mainly used for shipping and receiving these days. As you saw, we get a lot of packages. This floor houses the ballroom, the kitchen, the patent library, the chemistry lab, and some of the most impressive invention collections in the world."

"The Room of Firsts?" Vincent asked.

Calli looked shocked. "Yes, the Room of Firsts. How-ard's private invention museum. How did you know that?" she asked.

"I, ah, accidentally stumbled upon it looking for the bathroom the night before the contest."

"Oh, yes. The night of the accident. I felt so terrible about that. In all the years of holding the contest, we've never had that happen. What a terrible accident," Calli said.

"Yeah," Vincent said. "Accident." But Vincent knew better. He was sure the Spinowskis had broken his windless kite on purpose.

"Well, all's well that ends well, I always say. Where was I, now?"

"The Room of Firsts."

"Oh, yes. The Room of Firsts. A wonderful collection. The third floor has Fayman's physics lab, the model shop, and Grunt's computer lab."

"Grunt?" Vincent interrupted.

"Oh, yes. Grunt is a genius with computers and electronics. He used to work for NASA. Apparently he even helped put a man on the moon! Let's see, what else is on the third floor? Ah, the pottery room, complete with a walk-in kiln, and the metal shop."

"Metal shop?"

"Yes. Fayman uses it to fabricate little gears, parts, and whatnots."

"Does it have a blowtorch?" Vincent asked.

"Yes, I believe it has several."

"Cool." Vincent smiled.

"The fourth floor is the safe and the fifth floor—"

"The fourth floor is a safe?" Vincent interrupted again.

"Yup. Howard had the entire floor converted into a fireproof, burglarproof, storm-proof, waterproof, whatever-proof—safe. We're told it is the largest safe in the world. Although I've never seen it. To tell you the truth, I'm not even sure how to get to it."

Vincent wondered why Howard would need such a large safe. He wanted to ask her what she thought was in it. Money? Toys? Inventions? Gold? But instead, he nodded his head as if he understood the need for the world's largest hidden safe.

They stopped in front of the Room of Firsts.

"Normally I would take you through the room, but since you already saw it, maybe we'll just continue on upstairs?"

"I could spend all day in there," Vincent said, looking in through the door. Hundreds of inventions lined the walls of the room. The first wooden Pogo Stick invented by George Hansburg in 1919. The first Joy Buzzer invented by Soren Sorensen Adams in 1928. And Silly Putty, invented by James Wright in 1943. Then Vincent noticed the red velvet curtain hanging from the ceiling.

He had forgotten about the mysterious Tesla invention hidden behind the curtain.

"Ms. Callosum, can I ask you a question?"

"Oh, please call me Calli. Sure, go ahead. I'll do my best to answer it, but if it's about one of these inventions you may need to ask Howard."

"Oh. Okay. I'll wait and ask Howard." But Vincent had already asked Howard what was behind the curtain. Howard hadn't answered him.

"Well, if you're sure, then let's keep moving. Where was I?"

"The giant safe," Vincent offered.

"Yes, the fourth floor is the safe. The fifth floor—oh boy, the fifth floor. Do you know many artist types, Vincent?"

"Yes. Actually my mom was an artist. And my dad has worked in museums my entire life. He was the assistant director at the Met, until recently."

"Oh, really?"

"Yeah. But he left when they hired a new director. Now he's the director of a museum in Minnesota."

"Oh, well, then you fully under-stand the, the artist mentality. The fifth floor is home to Earl and Royal. Earl is a poet who writes all the copy for the Wondrous Whizzer Wishbooks. He also names all the toys. Royal Ducati is our resident artist, and he—"

"Royal Ducati? As in the Royal Ducati who illustrates the *Furious Jones* comic books?"

"One and the same. Are you a fan of Royal's work?"

"A huge fan. I have the first edition of every single *Furious Jones*."

"Well, Royal does all the art for the Wishbooks . . . when he's not drawing *Furious Jones*," Calli said.

"Wow." Vincent couldn't believe he was about to meet Royal Ducati.

Calli opened the door to the third floor. "They're both very nice men, and they do amazing work, but they rarely see eye-to-eye. Together, they're responsible for the creation of the Wondrous Whizzer Wishbooks.

"They've created twenty Wishbooks over the years. Each one a spectacle of invention, story, and art. The Smithsonian even has an entire collection of Wishbooks in its archives. But it's never easy. They're fire and water, those two." Calli stopped. "And the sixth floor is Howard's private residence."

She suddenly looked serious. "I think you'll find Whizzer Toys to be a fun place to work. We have a good time around here, and don't have many rules. In fact, there is only one rule. No one is allowed on the sixth floor. No one."

"Okay," Vincent said.

"I've never even been up there in all these years. That's Howard's and Howard's alone."

"Sure. No problem."

"Hey, sport." Fayman walked up behind Calli. "Check it out." He handed Vincent a football. "It's one of our newest inventions."

Vincent immediately dropped it.

"Oh boy, I'm sorry. I hope I didn't break it." Vincent bent down to pick it up. But he couldn't. The ball popped out of his hand. Embarrassed, he knelt down and tried to scoop it up with both hands. Fayman started laughing.

"Okay, okay. That's enough," Calli said. "Fayman is working on one of our newest novelty balls, the Fumble/Fumble Football. There is no way for you to grab that ball, Vincent."

"Unless you know the secret." Fayman winked at

Vincent, reached down, and picked up the football, no problem.

"Awesome! I would love to show that to my friends at my old school. It would be so much fun to watch Jeff Benz drop the ball every time." Vincent smiled at the thought of the six-foot sixth grader unable to catch a football.

"Well, the way things are going around here, that'll be a while," Fayman said as he walked back into his lab.

"You'll have to excuse Fayman. Again. He's been a little frustrated lately. It's been a while since we put out a new Wishbook," Calli said.

"So why don't you?"

"At the moment, we don't have enough toys for a Wishbook. We like to have about fifty new toys in each Wishbook."

"How many do you have?" Vincent asked.

"Ten. We only have ten new toys since the last Wish-book was published three years ago."

"Well, you can have my Pop Tunz and windless kite… if it helps," Vincent offered.

"That's very kind, Vincent. Now we're up to twelve." Calli smiled and started walking down the hall. Vincent followed. He was curious.

"How long does it take Mr. Whiz to invent fifty toys?"

"Well, in the old days Howard could invent fifty toys a year." She laughed. "Sometimes fifty toys a month. There was a time that we couldn't keep up with all of his ideas. But Howard has slowed down quite a bit in the last couple of years." Calli stopped walking and turned toward Vincent.

"Howard and I always start our day by eating

breakfast together at seven-thirty sharp. We used to use the time to review his latest inventions and decide which toys to build first. There were mornings when Howard would come downstairs with two or three new inventions that he had whipped up in the middle of the night. But for the last couple of years we just eat breakfast. Then Howard goes back upstairs. Or he spends the day tinkering in the Room of Firsts. He still shows up every morning at seven-thirty sharp, but he hasn't brought an invention down in over a year now."

Vincent thought about his old attic lab and his note-books full of ideas. With Fayman's help, he was sure they could make enough toys for a new Wishbook. His eyes watered as he remembered Danger Boy on the news. He had to get his inventions back. And fast.

"Oh, I'm sorry. I didn't mean to sound so gloomy.

Everything will be fine. Howard is an amazing man and I'm sure he still has enough ideas in him to fill several more Wondrous Whizzer Wishbooks. Hey, let's go upstairs and introduce you to Royal and Earl."

They climbed two flights of stairs to the fifth floor.

"That's strange," Vincent thought. There wasn't even a door to the fourth floor. How did Mr. Whiz get to the safe? And how was it possible that Calli didn't even know where it was, after all these years?

Calli opened the door to the long hallway on the fifth floor.

"Royal? Earl? I want you to meet someone," Calli yelled.

No one answered. They walked down the hallway and Calli poked her head into a couple of offices.

"It looks like they're not here. Well, you'll have to meet them later," Calli said as she pointed to an office. "Here you go. You can use this office."

Vincent looked in and saw a large wood desk covered with toys.

"My own office?" he asked.

"Yup. It's all yours. Why don't you get settled in and I'll go see if I can find those guys. Feel free to look around."

Vincent took a few minutes to organize the toys on his desk. And then he spent most of the day in the Room of Firsts.

MINNESOTA CALLING

16

Ring, ring. Ring, ring.

Ring, ring. Ring, ring.

"Hey, Aunt Bonnie? I think the phone is ringing," Vincent said.

"Oh, no, dear. That bird of yours is just trying to trick us. He's been doing it all night, haven't you—you little dickens." Aunt Bonnie poked her finger in the cage. Nikola used her finger to scratch his head.

Ring, ring. Ring, ring.

Ring, ring. Ring, ring.

"I really think it's the phone," Vincent said, trying to sound as polite as possible.

"Did you know that this bird of yours can tell jokes? Oh my goodness. He told me a knock-knock joke while you were in the other room. Now, let's see . . . how did it go?"

Ring, ring. Ring, ring.

Ring, ring. Ring, ring.

Vincent got up from the couch and walked to the phone.

"Hello? Hello?" He had missed the call.

"I told you, it's this amazing bird of yours," Aunt Bonnie said while singing *Pretty bird. Pretty bird* toward Nikola. "You know your uncle Ernie always wanted a parrot. Or was it a falcon?"

Ring, ring. Ring—

Vincent grabbed the phone.

"Hello?"

"Hey, buddy. How's it going? How was your first day on the big job?"

Vincent didn't realize how homesick he was until he heard his dad's voice.

"Hi, Dad! It was pretty good."

"Did you guys make any great new inventions today?"

"No, not really. I just kind of met everyone. And got set up. They gave me my own office, though."

"Wow! Look at you. Eleven years old and

you've already got your very own office. I'm proud of you. Soon you'll be running the place."

"I don't know about that, Dad."

"How is your Aunt Bonnie doing?" Norton asked.

Vincent looked over at Aunt Bonnie. She had Nikola out of his cage and was rubbing his belly.

"She's good. Everything is good."

"Knock-knock. Knock-knock," Aunt Bonnie said to Nikola.

"Just a minute, Vincent, Stella wants to talk to you," Norton said.

"Hey, Vincent. How's it going in the Big Apple?" Stella asked.

"Pretty good. Kind of a weird day."

"Did you tell Howard about the sketches?" Stella asked.

"No. Luckily I didn't see him today."

"What did they have you doing?"

"Nothing, really. I just kind of got a tour and met everyone." Vincent said. "Oh yeah, you know those *Furious Jones* comics books I like? Well, guess what? Royal Ducati, the guy who draws them, works at Whizzer Toys!"

"Really? Wow! Small world."

"Yeah, he does all the illustrations for the Wishbooks. When he's not doing that, he does the *Furious Jones* stuff. I got to meet him today. He was pretty cool."

"That's cool. It sounds like it wasn't too bad," Stella said.

"No. It was fine. But I'm not looking forward to seeing Howard."

"I'm sure it will be okay. Is that Nikola I hear in the background?" Stella asked.

"No. That's Aunt Bonnie."

ROYAL AND A POET NAMED EARL

17

Since their inception, over three hundred million Wishbooks have been printed in sixty-seven languages. The Wishbook has become part of the American landscape, treasured by children of all ages around the world. And Vincent Shadow was certainly no exception.

Once word got out that a new Wondrous Whizzer

Wishbook was coming, Vincent would check the mailbox daily. How big would it be? How many toys  would it have? How many boy toys? And which of the new inventions would Howard feature on the cover? The Wishbook always featured the most amazing of the new toy inventions on the cover. And they were always drawn in Royal's famous retro-futurist comic style. It was Howard's goal that his catalog be as entertaining as his toys. And it was.

The Wondrous Whizzer Wishbook was more like a comic book than a catalog. It had storylines, settings, recurring characters, and dialogue throughout each issue to help showcase each new toy. Earl had written each Wishbook. And Royal had illustrated.

Fans of the Wishbook might have assumed that Earl and Royal were of like minds to work so closely with each other and create something so wonderful. But nothing could have been further from the truth.

"Knock it off!" Earl yelled.

"*You* knock it off! You're the one that started it," Royal replied.

"You know, you're a 'royal' pain."

"Oh, like I've never heard that joke before. Did you think of that all by yourself, poet boy?" Royal grabbed an X-wing fighter off his desk and threw it over the six-foot wall that separated their offices.

"Hey, man, that almost hit my computer!" Earl grabbed the fighter and set it on his desk next to his other Star Wars action figures. "Thanks, Royal. That was the perfect addition to my collection."

Earl heard a squeak outside his office door. "Not this time, Royal," he thought. Earl quietly grabbed his eight-gallon Whizzer Shockwave from under his desk and tiptoed to the door. He kicked the door open and pulled back hard on the Shockwave's pressurized blast handle, sending a powerful vortex of water streaming directly at Vincent Shadow's head. Vincent was soaked. Again.

"Oh, man. Vincent! I'm sorry. I thought you were Royal."

Royal looked over the top of the office wall, laughing.

"Way to go, word man. You just soaked our new boy wonder."

"I'm starting to think I'll need a rain-coat to work here," Vincent said.

"I'm so sorry. Let's

get you some dry clothes before Calli sees you," Earl said.

Royal walked out of his office. He was dressed all in black. He was always dressed in black. "You'll have to excuse my colleague here. He tends to be a little jumpy."

Earl ran back into his office and emerged carrying a T-shirt with the words I'M A POET printed on the front. Earl had hundreds of I'M A POET T-shirts. They were the only shirts he ever wore. It drove Royal nuts.

"Here." Earl threw Vincent the T-shirt. "You can put this on. Calli called. She wants to see all of us down-stairs right now."

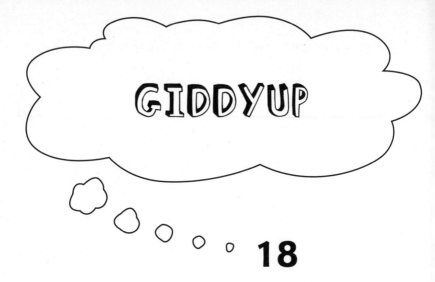

GIDDYUP

18

"Come on in, boys. Have a seat." Calli motioned to the two empty chairs in front of her desk. Vincent, Royal, and Earl rushed to get a seat.

"Oh my, what have you done to Vincent? Why is he wearing that ridiculous shirt?"

"Thank you," Royal said. "See, Earl, I'm not the only one that thinks it's stupid."

Vincent sat down in one of the open chairs.

"It's no problem. Really," Vincent replied.

"No problem?" Royal repeated as he tried to push Earl out of the way.

"What are you talking about?" Earl said. "It's a cool shirt." Earl grabbed Royal and yanked him backward. Earl jumped over the back of the open chair and landed with his legs crossed.

"You're too slow, painter boy. You'd better brush up on your chair-racing technique."

"Brush up?" Royal turned to Calli. "And you let him write for this company? With that ridiculous shirt and those crummy puns—'brush up.'"

"All right, you two. Let's try and behave. Today is a very special day," Calli said.

"Come on. This is technically Vincent's second day.

I think he needs to see how this place really operates. Speaking of operating, where is Fayman?" Royal asked.

"He's across the street, trying out the Hover Art prototype in the park," Calli said.

"Again?" Earl asked. "And you let him go? Alone?"

"I'm sure it'll be okay . . . this time." Calli suddenly looked concerned. "I hope he's smart enough to go to an area without people." She hesitated a second. "Anyway, back to the special-day part. I spoke to Howard this morning and"—Calli cleared her throat as if she were about to deliver bad news—"Howard would like me to send Vincent—upstairs."

"Upstairs?" Earl asked.

"To the sixth floor. Upstairs to the sixth floor," Calli repeated.

Earl stood up. "No! No way! Come on! Upstairs? Really?"

Royal jumped into the empty chair and smiled at Earl. Then he smiled at Vincent.

"Congrats, kid. That's awesome. No one has ever been upstairs. Hey, take pictures for us. Earl and I have this running bet. Maybe you can resolve it. See, I think Howard has a pet horse up there. I swear I can hear a horse walking around up there."

"No, no. I'm positive it's a llama. Or maybe an okapi," Earl said.

"What in the world is an *okapi*?" Royal asked.

"It's like a half-zebra, half-horse, half-deer thing found in the Congo. I saw it on the Discovery Channel."

"How would Howard have gotten this Congo hybrid horse-deer into the city and up to the sixth floor?"

"I don't know. But it is definitely not a horse. It's some sort of small ungulate."

"Listen," Calli said. "There's no horse. There's no llama. And there certainly is no mocha-pie thing."

Just then, Fayman walked into Calli's office. He was covered in red paint.

"What happened this time?" Royal asked.

Fayman shook his head. "It wasn't good."

"Did anyone get hurt?" Calli asked.

Fayman set what was left of the Hover Art prototype on Calli's desk. "No. Not this time. What's going on in here?"

"Vincent here is going upstairs," Royal said.

"Aw dude! I was kind of hoping he could work with me in the lab. You guys always get the interns upstairs. Do you know anything about gravity, kid?"

"No. Royal means Vincent is going all the way upstairs," Earl said.

"All the way upstairs?"

"Yes. Howard has asked Vincent to the sixth floor."

"Whoa. You are one lucky intern. Hey, let me know

if you see any wild boars running around up there, will ya?"

"Don't listen to them, Vincent," Calli said. "They're just jealous. Now, come with me. We'll get you a Whizzer Toys T-shirt and show you to the elevator."

THE SIXTH FLOOR

19

"Well, I'm sorry, Mr. Whiz, but you see I've got this obnoxious little sister. I'm sure she didn't deliberately destroy the only known documents that could've unraveled the mysteries surrounding the greatest scientific mind this world has ever known." Vincent felt terrible. He looked down at the floor. He knew he couldn't say that. As the elevator door opened onto the sixth floor, Vincent had no idea what he would say.

"Welcome back, Vincent!"

Howard G. Whiz was standing in front of Vincent wearing his usual white shirt, white jacket, white pants, white belt, white socks, and white shoes, and a white tie with the Eiffel Tower painted on it.

Howard shook Vincent's hand as he stepped off the elevator.

"Hello, Mr. Whiz. Thanks for having me back."

"Of course. I'm so excited you're here, Vincent." Howard took a deep breath. "We have so much work to do. And please, call me Howard."

"I'm excited to be here," Vincent said, looking down the long hallway lined with white ties.

"Oh, yes. My tie collection. I paint a new one every morning and then nail it to the wall every night. A pictorial diary of my life, if you will. There're over twenty thousand ties, I'm happy to say." Howard smiled as he slowly moved down the hallway.

"Well, come on in. I'll show you around. I was just about to feed the birds. Do you like birds, Vincent?"

"Very much. I have an African gray parrot."

"Wonderful birds, African grays. So smart."

"Yeah. Too smart, sometimes." Vincent smiled at the thought of Nikola's endless supply of jokes. "I named him after Tesla. And he's lived up to his name so far."

They walked down a long hallway with several closed doors. They entered a large windowless room at the end of the hallway. Blueprints and sketches covered every inch of the brick walls. Dozens of strange-looking machines cluttered most of the floor. Vincent recognized several of them as the Tesla inventions he had seen in the basement of the Met. A metal cage in a corner of the room stretched from the floor to the ceiling. And a well-worn workbench lined all four walls. The workbench was covered with toys. New toys. Toys that Vincent didn't recognize.

"Wow. What are all these?" Vincent carefully picked up a toy that looked like an airplane. He couldn't believe how light it was.

"This is my main lab. And that there, in your hand, is project 1623."

Vincent noticed a tag hanging from the plane that said 1623.

"These are my latest inventions. But I never name them. I find that names are like anchors. If you call something a football or an airplane, all you'll see is a football or an airplane. You close your mind to what else it could be. Besides, picking names is Earl's job— once the inventing is done."

Vincent walked along the bench looking at each toy. Each one perfectly crafted. Perfectly painted. And light! Vincent couldn't get over how light they were. He picked up number 1587. It didn't feel much heavier than his Pinewood Derby car.

"Are they just models, sir?"

"No. They're all finished prototypes."

"There must be over a hundred of them in here," Vincent said, looking around the room.

"One hundred and twenty. Or 121. Depending on how you look at it. Sixteen-twelve and 1613 kind of work together," Howard replied.

"So they work? They all work?" Vincent asked.

"No. None of them work yet. But I'm hoping that together we can change that. You see, I've gone and mixed up my dreams with Tesla's. But there is plenty of time for all of that later. Come on, let's go feed those birds before they get upset."

Howard navigated around the machines and slowly crossed the room toward the large metal cage. His cane clicked on the cement floor with each step.

"Sorry for the disarray. I don't get much company up here. Please watch your step."

Howard slid the metal cage door open. He was out of breath.

"After you," he said, motioning inside the cage with his cane.

Vincent and Howard climbed inside the cage. Howard pushed a button and pulleys turned, ropes moved, and the elevator started climbing toward the ceiling. It made a klop klop, klop klop sound as it climbed.

"I've been meaning to grease this old thing."

KLOP, KLOP.

KLOP, KLOP.

A hatch in the ceiling opened as the elevator rose. Sunlight poured in. Vincent shielded his eyes. Once they were on the roof, Howard pointed to a giant pigeon coop near the edge of the roof.

"Those are my babies."

"Pigeons?" Vincent asked.

"Yup. Racing Homers. Some of the fastest homing pigeons in the world. But I don't race them any more. I just enjoy their company. And watching them fly."

They crossed the roof to the coop. Howard struggled to pull the lever on the side. "Would you mind, Vincent?"

Vincent pulled the lever down and feed poured into the troughs.

"How's that cousin of mine?"

"Cousin?" Vincent forgot for a moment that his favorite teacher and Howard were cousins. Vincent was still thinking about the toys in Howard's lab. There were more than enough for a new Wishbook.

"Oh, Mr. Dennis. He's good."

"I imagine Dennis is a good teacher," Howard said.

"He is. We all like, um, Dennis." Dennis? Was Dennis Mr. D's first name? Vincent had always assumed it was his last name.

"Dennis used to spend his summers here, you know. Years ago. He helped Royal with the Wishbook art. He even helped with the toys, occasionally. He wasn't a half-bad inventor."

Howard pushed the lever back up and the feed stopped flowing.

"That ought to hold them for a while," he said as he turned and looked out over Central Park. "I never get tired of this view. I love this city."

"Me too. I miss it." Vincent said.

"So much history. So much energy. Speaking of energy, did you receive the copy of the Tesla notebooks I sent?"

Copies? Vincent was thrilled to hear the word *copies*. Maybe they weren't the originals. Maybe his obnoxious little sister hadn't ruined priceless historical treasures after all.

"Yes, I did. But—I'm not sure how to tell you this—but I'm afraid my sister accidentally ruined some of them. Actually, most of them, sir."

"Ruined them?"

"She colored little pink bunnies and puppies and stuff all over them." Vincent felt sick. "She didn't mean to. I mean, I'm sure she wouldn't have if she knew how important they were. I—" Vincent stopped. What could he say?

Howard roared. He laughed so hard Vincent was worried he would fall over.

"Oh, pink bunnies! That's priceless!"

Howard sat down on the edge of the building. He wiped the tears from his eyes.

"Maybe that's the missing piece, Vincent. Pink bunnies and puppies. It's as good as anything I've got."

"So you're not mad, sir?"

"Mad? Why? Oh my, you thought those were the original sketches? Oh, you poor boy. You must have been sick. No, no. She would have to wait almost five thousand years to draw on the originals. The originals are buried in a time capsule a few miles from here." Howard pointed north. "No, I have copies. Copies of what, though, I'm not sure. I have spent years of my life trying to figure out what those Tesla machines do. Every time

I think I'm close . . . well, it proves to be another dead end." Howard paused and wiped his eyes again.

"Oh, Vincent. This inventing thing is a young man's game. I'm glad you're here." Howard leaned on his cane, trying to stand up. "I'm kind of tired today. What do you say we take a look at Mr. Tesla's inventions tomorrow?"

"That sounds great," Vincent said.

THE GREAT WAVE

20

Vincent sat up in bed and looked at the
clock. Four forty-two AM. It was pointless to try to
sleep any more. Aunt Bonnie would be in to wake him
in just a few minutes. He grabbed a shirt out of his suitcase and hoped it would stay dry. He uncovered Nikola's cage.

"Good morning, buddy," Vincent said. He sat down

on the bed to put his shoes on. "You know, I met some pretty cool birds yesterday."

"Pretty bird. Pretty bird," Nikola said.

Vincent was thinking how great it would be to live in New York again. And how much fun it would be to have a rooftop for—

"Falcons." Aunt Bonnie burst into the room. "I'm pretty sure your uncle Ernie wanted falcons. Not parrots."

"Oh, yeah. Well, falcons are cool too."

"Yes, but messy. I don't think those birds of prey would make as good a pet as your little Nikola here."

"Right," Vincent agreed.

"Well, you're up early. Big day at the office today?"

"Yes, kind of. Mr. Whiz and I are going to start in on a new project together."

"Well then, you'll need a good breakfast. I'll go mix up some milk and pancakes for you."

"Great. Hey, Aunt Bonnie. Is it okay if I hang out with you at the museum until about eight o'clock? Nobody really gets to Whizzer until about eight o'clock."

"Oh, that will be just fine. Oh boy, I'd love the company and I know everyone would love to see you." Aunt Bonnie turned and walked to the kitchen.

Vincent sat on the bed thinking about what Howard had said: "I've gone and mixed up my dreams with Tesla's." He pulled Howard's letter out of his backpack: "... *I believe you may be the only person who can help unravel Tesla's secrets ... he claimed to have working prototypes ... I have those prototypes ... I have enclosed all of Tesla's notebooks ... Tesla's secret lies within these pages!*"

Vincent wondered why Howard had become so obsessed with Tesla. Vincent would have loved to see the Tesla inventions work as much as anyone, but Howard had a room full of new toys. Why not work on those first? Why not put out a new Wishbook?

"No way. No, no, no. This can't be young Mr. Shadow. No way. You're way too big to be little Vinny Shadow," the Met's security guard said as he held the door open for Vincent and Aunt Bonnie.

"Hi, Mr. Wooler," Vincent said.

"It's been too long, my friend. How is your dad doing?"

"He's fine." The security guard's German shepherd suddenly leaped up on Vincent and started licking his face.

"Well look at that. Addy remembers you. How old are you now, Vincent? I bet you and old Addy here must be about the same age."

"I'm eleven."

"Oh, boy. You've got her beat by two years. And good morning to you, Miss Bonnie," the guard said.

"Well, John, you're going to be seeing a lot of Vinny this summer," Aunt Bonnie said.

"Is that so?"

"Yes. He's working across the street at Whizzer Toys this summer."

"Oh, right, right. I heard something about you winning a contest. Congratulations, Vincent."

Vincent was on his knees petting the dog. "Thanks."

"Hey, Vincent," the guard said, sitting down on a small stool. "How about doing me a favor? I need to sit here and let everyone in to work. How about you take old Addy here for a walk around the museum and give her some exercise?"

Vincent looked up at Aunt Bonnie.

"That's fine with me, hon. It'll give me a chance to get the coffee going. And you can get reacquainted with the old place. Vincent used to spend a lot of time here, you know."

"Oh, yes. I remember, I remember," the guard said.

Vincent stood up and took the leash from the guard and started walking up the stairs with Addy. He knew just where he wanted to go.

"Okay. We'll be back in a bit." Vincent said.

Vincent had practically been raised at the Met. He knew every room. Every hallway. Every nook and cranny. And the Met had a lot of nooks and crannies. Vincent never liked walking around the Met alone when it was closed, though. It was spooky. But he felt just fine with his very own guard dog.

Vincent and Addy walked up the long marble staircase to the second floor. They turned right at the top of the stairs and headed to the Far East Art wing.

As soon as he turned the corner he knew something was wrong. He could usually see the tips of the waves on his mother's favorite painting from the top of the stairs. But there were no waves. As he got closer he saw a sign hanging where his mother's favorite painting had been. It said, TEMPORARILY ON LEAVE.

He looked around the room and noticed that most of the paintings in the room had been replaced with the same sign.

"What's going on here, girl?" Vincent said, patting Addy on the head. Vincent and his mom had spent countless hours sketching in this room. But now most of their favorite paintings were gone.

Vincent and Addy walked back downstairs.

"Hey, Mr. Wooler! Where did the *The Great Wave off Kanagawa* and the other Asian ink blocks go?"

"What? Oh, did you see a temporarily on leave sign on the wall?"

"Yeah."

"Oh, yeah. Lot of folks around here getting upset about that. Mr. Jilliver, the new museum director, he has seen fit to loan out many of the museum's pieces to private collections for cash. I think most of that Far East art is in a Las Vegas casino right now. Yes, it's causing a big uproar. A lot of people come from all over the world to see their favorite paintings and find that same sign you did. I hear about it all day. Got a lot of people mad. Including the chairman of the board. I heard he's not too happy with—"

Mr. Wooler was interrupted by someone pounding on the door.

"Mr. Jilliver! Good morning, sir," the guard said as he jumped off the stool and pushed the door open.

"Good morning, John. Boy, what a mess across the street," Mr. Jilliver said as he wiped his feet on the rug.

"What do you mean, sir?"

"There are reporters and police cars blocking the streets out there. I hope they don't clog the streets all day." Mr. Jilliver walked up the stairs.

Mr. Wooler and Vincent looked out the door and saw a crowd gathered in front of the Carlisle.

"I wonder what's going on?" Mr. Wooler asked.

"I heard someone say that toy inventor guy died in his sleep last night," Mr. Jilliver replied.

Vincent felt faint. He handed Addy's leash to Mr. Wooler and ran out the door. Flashing red lights filled his watering eyes as he ran down the sidewalk toward the Carlisle.

THE BEST MEDICINE

21

Vincent's entire family came to New York to be with him for Howard's funeral. Vincent's dad was worried that losing Howard, so soon after losing his mother, would be more than Vincent could handle. They were all gathered at Aunt Bonnie's the morning of the funeral, trying to cheer Vincent up.

"And you know what else was a little different about your uncle's funeral?" Aunt Bonnie asked.

"What's that?" Norton replied.

"All the picture-taking. The Finnish take a lot of pictures at funerals. Now you don't see that every day. No, sir."

"No, you don't," Norton replied.

"Of course the rest of the funeral was pretty straightforward. You know, dinner after, and everything else."

Vibs was walking around the room, obviously awestruck by the number of salt and pepper shakers in Aunt Bonnie's salt-and-pepper-shaker collection.

"This really is an amazing collection," Vibs said as she picked up a set of lighthouse-shaped salt and pepper shakers.

"Oh, thanks, hon. Those there really light up," Bonnie said.

"Really?" Vibs sounded surprised.

"Oh yeah." Aunt Bonnie walked over and twisted

the tops of the shakers and a beacon of light emanated from each.

"Oh, you know that Finns won't hand a salt or pepper shaker to you directly? That's true. I learned that at Uncle Ernie's funeral too. If you ask them to pass a shaker to you, they will set it in front of you, but never hand it directly to you. That's absolutely true."

Vibs set the lighthouse down. "Oh, you don't say."

"Nope. That's just how they do it," Bonnie replied.

Vincent looked at his dad and smiled. Maybe he was feeling a little better.

THE SALUTE

22

Word of Howard's death quickly spread around the world. Mr. Dennis decided that the Carlisle, home to both Howard and Whizzer Toys for over forty-three years, would be the perfect place to say good-bye to Howard.

Earl smiled as he looked down at the others. "I've been asked to say a few brief words. And when it comes to Howard, I can think of more than just a few words.

But 'kind,' 'passionate,' 'loyal,' 'brilliant,' and 'friend' would be near the top of the list. As many of you know, Calli, Royal, Grunt, and I have had the privilege of working with Howard for a very long time now. Most of our lives, really."

"And I couldn't imagine better people to spend it with. If you knew Howard, you knew he was a simple man. He wore the same outfit every day."

The crowd laughed.

"And he had a simple desire to bring joy to the world through the magic of toy inventing. And no one did it better than Howard. If you knew Howard, you would also know that he wouldn't want us to be sad now. Rather, he would want us to rejoice and celebrate his life and the wonderful toys he brought into this world. In other words, he would want us to play. So—"

Earl bent down and picked up a classic Whizzer Mega Fizzer.

"Royal and Calli are passing out Mega Fizzers. Please join us in honoring Howard with a twenty-one-shot Whizzer Mega Fizzer salute."

Hundreds of people had made their way to New York to say good-bye to the world's greatest toy inventor. Fans, friends, people old and young packed the Carlisle's second-floor ballroom. A tear ran down Vincent's face as Mr. Dennis handed him a Whizzer Mega Fizzer. His father held his own Whizzer Mega Fizzer in one hand and reached out to Vincent with the other.

"Okay. On three, everybody. ONE! TWO! THREE!"

A tremendous *POP* came from the Carlisle as they all shot their Whizzer Mega Fizzers at the same time. And then foam started to fill the room.

POP!

POP!

POP!

Billows of colored foam filled the room. The foam

was ankle-deep by the thirteenth shot. Past Vincent's waist by the eighteenth. The foam was almost touching the ceiling and a rainbow of color was flowing down the staircase by the end of the salute. People were swishing, swooshing, blowing, and sculpting the foam. Adults were spinning and skipping through the techno-colored suds. Vincent turned to Stella.

"Seems like the perfect way to say good-bye."

THE WILL

23

"Look at this mess," Earl said. **"There** must have been four or five hundred people here."

"I say we forget about the mess until Monday and order some pizza. I'm starving," Fayman said, kicking what was left of the foam on the floor of the ballroom.

"I second that. As long as it's from DiCamillo's," Royal added.

A man in a suit appeared at the top of the grand

staircase. "Excuse me. Is there a Mr. Dennis Gordon Whiz here?"

"Well, I haven't been called that in a long time," Mr. Dennis said. "I'm Dennis Whiz. How can I help you?"

"My name is Mr. Potts. I was Howard's attorney. And let me start by saying how sorry I am for your loss."

"Thank you."

"I have here Howard's last will and testament." Mr. Potts reached inside his briefcase and handed Mr. Dennis a thin envelope. "It's very simple. As Howard's only living relative, you will inherit his entire estate. That is the Whizzer Toy Company, the Carlisle, and everything in it. Congratulations, Mr. Whiz."

"What? I inherit what? That can't be."

"Everything, sir," Mr. Potts said. "You've inherited everything."

Mr. Dennis sat down on the wet floor. "What am I gonna do with a toy company?"

"Well then, I guess this is now your mess to clean up," Fayman said.

"A toy company? What do I know about running a toy company?"

"There's not much to it." Calli tried to reassure him. "Whizzer practically runs itself."

"Yeah, it runs itself just fine with Calli's eighty-hour workweeks. But I wouldn't worry about it too much, Dennis. You need toys to run a toy company. And we ain't got no toys."

"FAYMAN!" Calli yelled.

"No, he's right, Calli," Royal said. "You have to admit it is a problem. And even if we had toys, who's going to invent the new stuff going forward? I hate to say it, but—"

Vincent cut Royal off. "There are toys. Lots of them."

"What are you talking about, Vincent?" Calli asked.

"Upstairs. In Howard's lab. He has lots of new toys. Enough to fill two Wishbooks."

"Seriously?" Fayman sounded skeptical.

"Seriously. I saw them myself." Vincent decided not to mention the part about the toys not working yet.

"Well! Thataboy, Howie!" Mr. Dennis jumped to his feet. "Come on. Let's go up to the sixth floor and get a look at these amazing new Whizzer toys!"

A LONG DAY

24

"So this is what he did with all of those ties. Unbelievable," Royal said as he examined row after row of ties. "I remember most of these."

"Ah, I remember the day Howard wore this one," Earl said, pointing to a tie that was painted all black.

"Oh, yeah," Royal said. "The 1977 blackout tie."

"Well, my cousin had style. That's for sure," Mr. Dennis said.

"The toys are in the room at the end of this hallway." Vincent led Calli, Royal, Earl, Fayman, Mr. Dennis, and his dad down the long hallway into Howard's main lab.

"Oh, my," Calli said as they entered the lab cluttered with Tesla devices and sketches. Then she saw the 120 toys carefully lined up on the workbench surrounding the room. "Look at this. How did he— Why didn't he—" Calli was shaking. "I don't think I'm ready for this." She ran out of the lab.

"I'll go make sure she's okay," Earl said, running after Calli.

"Wow, Vincent. You weren't kidding. Look at all of these toys," Fayman said.

"What do you think all these machines do?" Mr. Dennis pointed to the Tesla devices covering most of the floor.

"Probably more of Nikola Tesla's stuff," Fayman

said. "Howard was obsessed with Tesla for the last few years."

"Hey, we had some of these machines at the Met. Remember, Vincent?" Norton asked.

"Yeah, Dad. Most of the stuff here was at the Met."

"What was it doing at the Met?" Mr. Dennis asked.

"All this stuff was discovered in an old hotel storage room about a year ago. We cleaned it up and helped auction it off." Norton paused. "I used to be the assistant director at the Met. Howard paid ten million dollars for all this stuff."

"Yes, and there's more where that came from," Royal said. "Howard has some Telsa artifacts downstairs in the Room of Firsts. And all of those boxes on the first floor are full of Tesla stuff."

"And don't forget the safe. Who knows what he has in the safe," Fayman added, picking up one of the toy prototypes. "Look at these things. They're amazing!

Who knew Howard could build proto- types like this? I could've been out of a job."

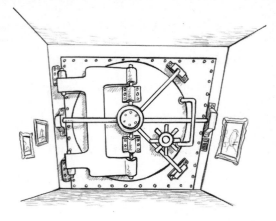

"You still could be," Royal replied.

"Nonsense. We're going to get through this—some- how." Mr. Dennis tried to smile.

Royal picked up one of the inventions. "It's so light. What do you think this thing does?"

"I don't know. Is there an on button?" Fayman asked.

"I don't see any." Royal picked up another prototype. "Maybe they're just models of things he wanted you to build, Fayman."

"No," Vincent insisted. "Mr. Whiz told me they were finished toys."

"But look, Vincent." Fayman flipped over one of the prototypes. "They don't have any buttons. Or switches. They don't seem to do anything." He flipped over two more prototypes. "And they're light because they don't have any batteries. There isn't even a place for a battery. I hate to say it, kid, but I don't think these things are real toys."

"No. Howard, I mean Mr. Whiz, specifically told me they were finished toys. But they didn't work yet."

"Okay, okay," Fayman said. Royal and Fayman both set the prototypes down.

"But I still think we're back to square one. A toy company with no toys." Fayman walked out of the room.

"Look at all these machines," Mr. Dennis said. "Howard clearly had a passion for Mr. Tesla's work. It would be a shame for all of these great inventions to remain hidden from the world. Norton, do you think the Met would be interested in a collection like this?"

"I'm sure a lot of museums would be interested in this collection. I'd be happy to help you."

"What? But Mr. D, you can't get rid of the Tesla inventions. Howard loved these." Vincent wanted to tell them about Howard's letter and their conversation on the roof. And the secret Tesla sketches now covered in pink bunnies. But he knew it was pointless. They would only think Howard had lost his mind. Vincent had to solve this on his own. He needed to figure out what the Tesla machines did—for Mr. Whiz.

"Now, Vincent, please. We should be going. This has been a long day for Mr. Dennis," Norton said.

"Ah, yes. It's been a long day for all of us. Let's meet back here tomorrow and look at all of this with fresh eyes. There's always more than one right answer. Right, Vincent?"

"I hope so, Mr. D."

UNCLE ERNIE'S FINNISH SECOND COUSINS

25

"**Good news, everybody. You're all** staying in New York for the rest of the week," Vincent said as he and his dad walked into Aunt Bonnie's living room.

Vibs, Gwen, and Stella were sitting on the couch. And Anna was sitting on the floor under a table full of salt and pepper shakers.

"What? What is Vincent talking about?" Vibs stood up.

"Well, dear, do you remember that exhibit of inventions I helped auction off last year? It turns out Howard Whiz not only bought those inventions, but many, many more like them. He has actually put together a very impressive collection. Well, Mr. Dennis doesn't know what to do with all that stuff, so I offered to stay and, and help him. Just for the week."

Vibs stared at Norton.

"I mean considering the situation . . . it seems like, ah, like the right thing to do. Maybe. And since Vincent obviously isn't going to have his summer internship, this would at least give him—"

"What?" said Vincent. "What do you mean I won't have my summer internship? Why can't I stay, Dad? Mr. Dennis is going to need all the help he can get. Who's going to invent all the new toys they need?"

"I don't even know if Whizzer Toys is going to stay in business, buddy. You heard what they said. They need a lot of new toys to keep going. Even if you stayed all summer, Vincent, I don't think—I mean, it's nice of you to want to help, but I'm afraid it's going to take more than one person to save Whizzer Toys."

"Howard was one person. And he *built* Whizzer Toys."

"Yeah, but—"

"And Calli told me Howard wasn't much older than me when he started it."

"But those were different times, Vincent."

"What does that even mean, Dad?"

"It means, let's just focus on helping Mr. Dennis with the things that we can do. Now. I can help him find a home for all the Tesla artifacts."

"They have a home. Whizzer Toys is their home." Vincent walked into the back bedroom and slammed the door.

Norton exhaled loudly. "Maybe we should just go back to Minnesota."

"Oh, nonsense. I won't hear of it," Aunt Bonnie said. "It's just been a long day for everyone. These things happen. They just happen. You can all stay right here.

I've plenty of room. And I would love the company. The more the merrier. And I'm sure Mr. Jilliver would be more than happy to let you work out of the museum while you help out this Mr. Dennis. At least I think he would. Everyone there misses you so much, Norton. It hasn't been the same since you left. No, no, no. Not the same."

Vibs looked around Aunt Bonnie's living room. It housed an impressive salt-and-pepper-shaker collection. There were hundreds, maybe even thousands of salt and pepper shakers.

"Oh, Aunt Bonnie. We couldn't possibly impose on you like that," Vibs said with an attempted smile.

"No imposition whatsoever. Once we had Uncle Ernie's Finnish second cousins stay with us for six years." Bonnie looked around the room. "Of course, I hadn't added the cat-shaped salt and pepper shakers then. So there was a bit more room. But, oh, those Finn boys were tall. Six and a half feet each! Even the little one. And they all fit. Yes sir. We were just fine. Of course, that Hessu was a bit odd. He slept up on the roof."

Gwen looked around the room. "I'll sleep on the roof," she offered.

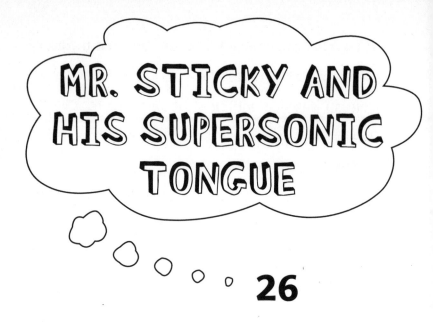

MR. STICKY AND HIS SUPERSONIC TONGUE

26

The next morning Vibs offered to take the kids to the Empire State Building, but Stella decided to spend the day helping Vincent at Whizzer Toys. Vincent and Stella could hear shouting coming from Fayman's lab as they walked down the hall.

"I'm telling you, Royal, we can't sell a log-rolling game," Earl said.

"Why not?" Royal asked. "We could put a big plastic log on rollers and the kids could try to roll each other off the log. It would be great fun. Kids would love it. All kids want to be logrolling lumberjacks. Oh hey! We could call it the Log-Jack game."

"It would be too dangerous. A kid could get hurt falling off the log. And how about we leave the product naming to me?" Earl said.

"Ah, there he is," Mr. Dennis said as Stella and Vincent walked in. "Just the man we need. Good morning, Vincent. Good morning, Stella. Does everyone here know Vincent's sister?" Mr. Dennis was standing at the far end of the room wearing a white lab coat. Fayman, Royal, and Earl were sitting around a large table.

"Yes. I met everyone at the funeral," Stella said sadly as she looked down at the floor.

"Ah, yes. Well, come on in, you two, and have a seat. We were just about to brainstorm new toy ideas. And, if everyone will remember, the first rule of brainstorming is that there are no wrong ideas." Mr. Dennis turned around and wrote LOG-JACK on a large whiteboard. "We'll have plenty of time to judge later. So shake off the negativity for now." Mr. Dennis's hands were a blur as he shook them in the air. "Come on, everyone, shake it off."

Stella's ring flew across the room as she shook her hands.

"Great. Let's start out slow. For now, let's just brainstorm until we come up with ten ideas. No matter how crazy they are, just throw 'em out there."

Royal started. "All right. I've said this before, but I'll say it again—I think it would be fun if we had an action figure with a super-long and super-sticky tongue. You would squeeze him and this thirty- or forty-foot tongue would shoot out. You could use the tongue to swing from buildings. Or capture bad guys. I could create a comic to go with it and we could call it Mr. Sticky and his Supersonic Tongue," Royal said.

Earl groaned.

"Good, good." Mr. Dennis wrote MR. STICKY AND HIS SUPERSONIC TONGUE on the whiteboard.

"Now, let's go with that. What else could we do with a supersonic tongue or something sticky?"

"We could make the tongue out of fruit snacks," Earl suggested. "And the little guy could actually be a fruit snack dispenser. Whenever you get hungry, you just grab the little guy, rip off a nice big piece of tongue, and enjoy." Earl stuck his tongue out at Royal.

"Good." TONGUE CANDY DISPENSER Mr. Dennis wrote, not realizing it was a joke. "Good. This is a great way to brainstorm. Keep working off each other's ideas. What else could we do?"

"We could maybe create super sticky foam balls? You could shoot the balls at someone and they would stick when they hit them," Stella offered.

"GREAT, Stella." Mr. Dennis was jumping up and down as he wrote SUPER GLUE BALLS on the board. "What else?"

"What if we take the little guy with the tongue," Fayman said. "But we make the tongue out of rubber. The guy would have this really long, fat rubber tongue hanging out of his mouth. And when you pull it—he burps. The harder the pull...the bigger the belch!"

"Yes!" Earl jumped up. "We would call them Belcher Bob!"

"Right on, right on. Now you got it. Keep going, keep going," said Mr. Dennis.

"Or maybe we call them Loud Mouths," Stella suggested. "You pull their tongues and they scream really loud. I mean REALLY REALLY loud. People would hear it twelve blocks away!"

"Or, what if you put the fake tongue in your mouth, but it was really a straw? You could stick this long fake tongue into a glass and drink through it," Earl suggested.

"Oh, hey, better yet. Instead of a tongue straw, what if we make vampire teeth straws? 'I want to suck your fruit juice,'" Fayman said in his best vampire accent.

"Okay, okay. This is good," Mr. Dennis said, trying to keep up with the ideas. "Let's move away from tongues for a moment. What else can we do? Vincent, we haven't heard from you yet. What great idea is simmering in that brain of yours? Give us a chance to play off one of your brilliant ideas, Vincent."

"Ah, how about the Pump-Up Pickup?" Vincent said.

"Oh, yes! Tell everyone about the Pump-Up Pickup," Mr. Dennis said while he wrote on the board.

"It's a truck with pumps that let you inflate the tires and turn the truck into a giant monster truck built in to the hubcaps." Vincent hoped Danger Boy hadn't already shown the idea on TV.

"Cool," Earl said.

"Hey, that's way cool," Royal agreed. "Maybe we could also build a line of monster trucks that have heat-seeking devices in them? They would attack you as soon as you took them out of the box."

"Wonderful! Look at that," Mr. Dennis added up the ideas on the whiteboard. "We had ten ideas in less than ten minutes." He was sweating.

"I really love your idea, Vincent. If you don't mind, I'm going to get started building the pickup," Fayman said.

"Great. One down and only thirty-nine more to go." Earl said.

"Thirty-eight more to go," Royal interjected. "Don't forget about Mr. Sticky and his tongue."

THOUGHTS OF PARIS

27

"That was kind of fun," Stella said as she and Vincent stepped onto the elevator. Vincent pushed the button for the sixth floor.

"You should be a toy inventor, Stella. You're really creative."

"No. I'm going to live in Paris and write bestselling, critically acclaimed novels that get translated into dozens of languages and are enjoyed by millions of people around the world."

"Oh. Well, if that doesn't work out, I'm sure Mr. D would hire you here."

"No, that's your thing, Vincent. Hey, why did Earl say 'Just thirty-nine more to go'?"

"That's how many new inventions they need for a Wondrous Whizzer Wishbook. Without thirty-nine more ideas, there probably won't be a Wishbook…or a Whizzer Toy Company."

"You probably have thirty-nine ideas in your old lab, Vincent. Why don't we just go talk to Mr. Spinowski and tell him that Danger Boy stole your toy ideas?"

"You met Spinowski. And you saw what he did to my kite. There is no way he's going to give us those ideas back. Especially to help Whizzer Toys stay in business.

Besides, without the notebooks, how would we even prove the inventions were mine?"

"Well, let's go talk to Danger Boy, then. We can get the notebooks back and get him to admit he stole them."

"How?"

"He's a little kid. We'll scare it out of him," Stella said, sounding defeated. "I'll scare it out of him. Come on Vincent, it's not right. You have to do *something*."

The elevator door opened and they stepped off onto the sixth floor.

"This way," Vincent said, pointing down the long hall.

"Whoa, look at all the ties."

Vincent spotted a tie with a kite painted on it. "Hey, that's the tie Mr. Whiz was wearing the night I met him!"

"This is amazing," Stella said. "What are they going to do with all of these?"

"I don't know."

Vincent noticed one of the doors in the hallway was open a crack. He stopped and slowly pushed open the door.

"Is this the way to the birds?" Stella asked.

"Not exactly."

"Vincent, we're just supposed to feed the birds. We could get in trouble."

"Relax, Stella. We should look around a little bit. What if Mr. Whiz had other pets that need feeding?"

A wall of floor-to-ceiling windows filled the room with light. There was a drafting table and a cart full of paints in front of the windows and a small bed in the corner.

"This must have been his bedroom," Stella said.

Vincent walked up to the closet and slid the door open. Dozens of white suits hung neatly on hangers.

"What are you looking for?" Stella asked.

"I don't know," Vincent replied.

Vincent noticed a tie on the drafting table. "That was the tie Howard was wearing the day he died." He picked up the tie. "Wonder why he painted the Eiffel Tower on it?"

"Maybe he was planning a trip to Paris."

"Maybe. Tesla lived in Paris before coming to America. Maybe he was going to look for more Tesla stuff."

Stella reached out and grabbed the tie from Vincent. "That's not the Eiffel Tower. The Eiffel Tower doesn't have a big ball on top of it like this."

Stella pointed to a large hemisphere painted onto the tower's trusses.

"Are you sure?"

"Trust me," Stella said. "I've dreamed of Paris my entire life."

Vincent took the tie and shoved it in his pocket.

"What are you doing? You can't just take that."

"I'm just going to borrow it for a bit. Look." Vincent pointed to the twenty thousand ties that lined the walls of the hallway. "No one is going to miss one tie, Stella."

"Ah, there you are. Great job today. Great job, you two," Mr. Dennis said, walking into the bedroom. "I think it was fate that brought you here, Vincent. Absolute fate. You're a young Howard Whiz. That toy idea was brilliant. Just brilliant. A few more of those and we'll be well on our way."

"Yeah. Ah, Mr. D? We have a problem. My dad is taking us back to Minnesota at the end of the week."

"What? Oh, no." Mr. Dennis sat down on Howard's bed. "Well, I guess that is a problem. But it does give us a couple more days. Maybe if we all work at it, we can come up with enough ideas before you two leave. Or at least get close. We shouldn't waste a moment, then." Mr. Dennis stood up. "Are you ready to go back downstairs and dream up some more toys?"

Vincent looked at Stella and then back at Mr. Dennis.

"There is another problem."

"What is it, Vincent?" Mr. Dennis sat back down.

Vincent paused. "Mr. D, I can't control my ideas. I don't really know how, or even where, my ideas come from. They just come. Bam! Whenever they want to—but lately, not so much."

"Oh, Mr. Shadow! You had me worried for a minute. Well, that's no problem. No problem at all. That just gives me a chance to do what I do best. Teach! Inspiration is all around you. You just have to look. Come on, let's get out of here." Mr. Dennis stood up and walked out of Howard's bedroom.

"Where are we going?" Stella asked.

"To cook up some creativity!"

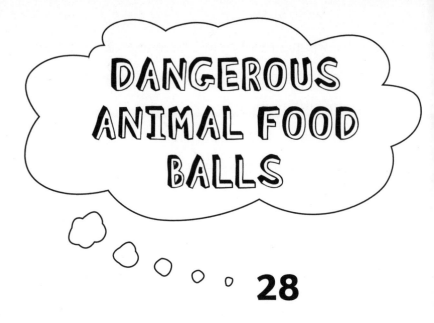

DANGEROUS ANIMAL FOOD BALLS

28

Mr. Dennis was digging through the Carlisle kitchen cupboards.

"What are we doing in here, Mr. D?" Vincent asked.

"We are going to create a recipe for great toy inventions, Mr. Shadow. That's what we're doing. Just as soon as I can find some things for us to work with."

"Okay." Vincent looked at Stella and shrugged.

Mr. Dennis jumped up on the counter and opened a door revealing an entire cupboard of cinnamon-flavored Pop-Tarts. Hundreds of boxes of Pop-Tarts.

"Ah, yes. I see Howard and Calli were still enjoying their morning Pop-Tarts."

"I love Pop-Tarts," Stella said.

"All right, then we'll use Pop-Tarts. Catch!" Mr. Dennis threw several boxes over his shoulder. He jumped off the counter. The smell of cinnamon filled the room as he ripped open the boxes.

"You see, Vincent? You can control your creativity. You just need someone to show you how. Let's start with a simple exercise." Mr. Dennis set a single Pop-Tart on the marble countertop.

"What is it?" Mr. Dennis asked.

Vincent looked at the Pop-Tart. He knew Mr. Dennis. He knew there was no way the answer would be "Pop-Tart."

"It's a Pop-Tart," Stella said.

"Right!"

Vincent was shocked.

"Right. It's indeed a Pop-Tart. Now, what *else* is it?"

"What do you mean?" Stella asked.

"I mean it is all in the way you look at it, you see."

Stella tilted her head. "I don't know. Still looks like a Pop-Tart, Mr. D."

"Yes, the kind people at the breakfast company decided to call it a Pop-Tart. And then it became a Pop-Tart. But it is more than that. Much more."

"It's delicious," Stella said.

Mr. Dennis picked it up and took a big bite of the breakfast bar. "Umm, yes. Yes, it is delicious." Several large crumbs fell from his mouth and stuck to his shirt. He threw more Pop-Tarts on the counter. "Now, what *else* are these things? Look at it differently. Remember, there are many right answers."

Vincent looked at the Pop-Tarts and then ripped open a box. He started building a house out of Pop-Tarts. "They're walls for building," he said. "And this"—Vincent pulled a pouch of frosting from the box—"this is the glue."

"YES! YES! An edible building set. That's exactly right." Mr. Dennis set a frosting pouch on the counter, looked around the room, and then grabbed a giant cookbook.

SMACK.

The frosting shot across the room as he hit the pouch with the book.

"It's a cannon," he declared.

Stella picked up the cookbook. She opened the book and placed a Pop-Tart between pages 253 and 254 and slammed it shut.

"It's a bookmark!"

"RIGHT! RIGHT! It is indeed a bookmark!" Mr. Dennis

said as a large chunk of Pop-Tart fell to the floor. "Well done."

Mr. Dennis spread frosting on top of a Pop-Tart, walked across the kitchen, and stuck it to the wall.

"It's art," he declared.

Vincent pounded several Pop-Tarts into a ball.

"It's food for dangerous animals. You know, when you can't get too close, you can just throw it to them," Vincent said as he threw the dangerous animal food ball across the kitchen. It flew over the counter and past the pantry, and reached the door- way at the exact same moment that Fayman

entered the kitchen. And the dangerous animal food ball exploded on Fayman's forehead.

No one said a word as Fayman wiped cinnamon from his eyebrows.

"Okay," he said, looking at Vincent. "We're even." He turned around and walked out.

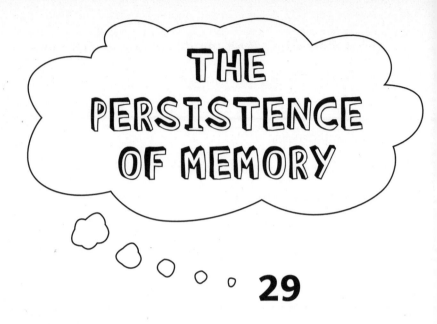

THE PERSISTENCE OF MEMORY

29

Vincent and Stella opened Aunt Bonnie's kitchen cupboard, looked around, and grabbed a box of spaghetti noodles and a jar of olives. Vincent closed the cupboard, pulled a handful of noodles out of the box, and placed them on the kitchen table. "Okay," he said, "What else can this be?"

Stella stuck a noodle into an olive. "It could be a min-iature flagpole."

"Yeah," Vincent said, sticking several more noodles into the olive. "Or a satellite."

Vincent pushed the satellite to the middle of the table and put his head down. "This is pointless."

"What's pointless?" Stella asked.

"This," Vincent said, pointing to the olive. "Trying to save Whizzer Toys. All of it. It's just pointless. We can't save a major toy company with—with an olive satellite."

"You're right."

Vincent lifted his head. He had expected one of Stel-la's pep talks.

"You're absolutely right, Vincent. That's why we need to go get your toys back. You've got enough toys to save the company. I don't get it."

"But who's going to believe they're mine?"

"We'll go over there with Mr. D. How else would you know about the secret attic lab if it wasn't yours?"

"That's true."

"And besides, you put your initials on every drawing!"

"Yeah, I did." Vincent rubbed his eyes. "Okay. We'll talk to Mr. D tomorrow."

"Now you're talking!" Stella said.

"Talking about what?" Gwen asked as she walked into the kitchen.

"Talking about dinner," Stella answered. "What's for dinner?"

"I don't know, but I'm starving." Gwen opened the refrigerator, looked in, and closed it. "MOM! What's for dinner? I'm starving."

"You may be hungry, but you are not starving," Vibs

said, walking into the kitchen. "Vincent, what are you doing? Clean up this mess before your Aunt Bonnie gets home."

"Oh, hey. Can I have that?" Gwen asked, pointing to the olive.

"Sure."

Gwen popped the satellite in her mouth and took a bite of the uncooked noodle. "Tasty," she said.

"Norton, honey?" Vibs yelled. "What do you want to do about dinner?"

"Oh, no dinner for me, hon. I actually have a meeting up at MOMA in twenty minutes."

"MOMA?" Vibs asked.

"The Museum of Modern Art. They may be interested in the Tesla collection."

"Hey." Vincent ran into the living room. "Can I go with you, Dad?"

"Sure, sport. Get your shoes on."

Norton stood on the curb with his hand in the air, trying to hail a taxicab. Vincent missed taxis. He hadn't seen a taxi the entire time he was in Minnesota.

"Here we go," Norton said as a yellow-and-black taxi pulled up to the curb. Norton opened the door for Vincent.

Vincent slid across the seat and looked out the window. Norton climbed in and closed the door.

"The Museum of Modern Art, please," Norton said to the cabdriver. He turned to Vincent. "How was everyone at Whizzer Toys today? Are they doing okay?"

"Yeah, I guess so. We tried to do some brainstorming today."

"Well, that must have been fun. That's right up your alley."

"Yeah? I don't know. I didn't have much. Stella was good, though."

"Oh, come on, champ," Norton said. "You're being too hard on yourself. You're always filling those notebooks with ideas and drawings. I'm sure you were fine."

"I don't know," Vincent said.

"Anyway, that happens to all great artists and writers," Norton said. "Sometimes you're going to get writer's block. Or, um, inventor's block . . . as it were."

Norton paused. "It even happened to your mom from time to time."

"Really?"

"Sure. I remember she went three months once without working on a single project. And I'm not just talking paintings. I mean no sketches, no drawings, nothing." Norton chuckled. "And you know how your mother was. That was not normal for her. She was always creating something or another."

Vincent smiled.

"Hey, you know what she used to do when she was stuck for ideas?"

"No, what?"

"She always consulted Dalí."

"Dalí?"

"Yeah. Salvador Dalí. She would sit in front of a Dalí painting for hours. It was almost like they spoke to her."

Vincent noticed his dad's eyes watering. "And I think they did—speak to her." Norton wiped his eyes and smiled. "She would joke that she saw things differently after spending time with Dalí."

"I never knew she liked Dalí," Vincent said. "We spent most of our time in the Far East wing of the Met."

"Oh, I think it was something she preferred to do alone. She loved the surrealists and Postimpressionists. Van Gogh was another one of her favorites. She loved *The Starry Night* by van Gogh. You know she named you after him?"

"Yeah, she told me." Vincent smiled. He hadn't heard his father mention his mom like that in a long time.

ALARMING

30

The taxi pulled up in front of the Museum of Modern Art, just a mile south of the Met and the Carlisle. Norton handed the cabdriver five dollars and they climbed out.

"Okay, I've got to meet with these guys for a little bit. Why don't you look around the museum and I'll come find you when I'm done?" Norton said as they walked into the museum's stark white lobby.

"Sure, Dad."

"Hey, Vincent," Norton yelled as he crossed the lobby. "I think van Gogh's *Starry Night* is on the fifth floor. And so is Dalí's melting clocks. Your mom loved that painting too."

☆ ☆ ☆

Vincent laughed when he saw Van Gogh's *Starry Night*. He realized he had seen the painting before. But not van Gogh's version. He had watched his mom recreate the painting in finger paints years earlier. She had dumped small piles of yellow paint on the paper and pushed her finger through it, creating brilliant thick stars atop a dark blue sky. Vincent still had the painting. As he stood a few inches away from van Gogh's *Starry Night*, he wondered if van Gogh had used his fingers to make his thick, brilliant stars.

Vincent walked past primal paintings by Paul Gau-

guin and strange dis-
torted figures created
by Pablo Picasso. And
then he saw the clocks.
There, hanging on the
wall, was *The Persis-*

tence of Memory by Salvador Dalí.

He stood in front of the small-framed painting. The brushstrokes were much finer than van Gogh's. Almost invisible. And the colors were duller. The melting clocks actually looked more like soft rubber pocket watches. There was a large watch melting and running off the edge of a table. Another watch hung over a tree branch. Another was melting on top of a strange object on the beach. And a fourth watch was lying facedown covered with ants. Vincent thought about what Mr. Dennis had said about Salvador Dalí and the surrealists. How they would look for connections between seemingly unconnected things. He wondered what the painting meant. What did Dalí want him to see? What had his mother seen?

Vincent stepped back and stared at the painting. He liked the van Gogh better. Why were three of the watches on Dalí's painting melting? And why was the other one covered with ants? It didn't make any sense. Was Dalí painting things he dreamed?

Vincent noticed a fly standing on the face of the largest watch. The fly was casting a giant shadow. But the shadow seemed to be growing. Vincent moved closer. He heard a loud buzzing sound as the fly's shadow quickly engulfed the entire painting. "Oh, no," Vincent said out loud as everything around the painting went black.

Sparks leaped from the top of the watch. The face of the watch melted away and the numbers straightened as if to form legs. The legs started to stretch and climb toward the sky.

"HEY! GET AWAY FROM THERE, KID!"

Vincent felt someone grab his shoulder. He spun around and fell to the ground. The watches were gone.

"What are you doing? You can't touch the paintings."

Vincent looked up to see a burly security guard. "What?"

"You can't touch the paintings," the guard repeated.

Vincent looked over at the Dalí painting, which was now hanging crooked on the wall.

"Oh geez. I'm so sorry. I guess I got dizzy and—and I must have fallen into the painting. Is it okay?"

"Yeah, it looks fine," the guard said, straightening the painting. "You're lucky, kid."

Three more men dressed in suits ran into the room.

"What's going on? Is everything okay?"

"Yeah, everything's fine. This kid accidentally got too close to the Dalí. It's okay. We've talked." The guard helped Vincent to his feet. "Are you okay, kid?"

"Yeah, I'm fine. Just a little dizzy, that's all. I haven't eaten dinner. Maybe that's it."

"Who are you here with?" one of the men asked.

"My dad."

"Well, where is he?"

"Ah . . . he's downstairs in a meeting." Vincent immediately regretted telling them where his dad was. He hadn't seen his dad this angry since the time Vincent had borrowed the ball bearings from his favorite fly-fishing reel. It took a lot to get his dad angry. But he was pretty sure setting off the silent alarm at the Museum of Modern Art would do the trick.

IN TROUBLE

31

Vincent and Norton walked into Aunt Bonnie's apartment. Vincent raced to the back bedroom and closed the door.

"What's that all about?" Vibs asked.

"Oh, don't even ask," Norton said. "I've never been so embarrassed in all my life."

"What happened?"

"Vincent set off the museum's alarm while I was in my meeting."

"Well, I'm sure it was an accident, honey," Vibs said.

"Of course it was an accident. But he knows better. The kid has practically been raised in museums. He knows better."

"How did the meeting go?" Vibs asked.

"Good, actually." Norton sat down on the couch. "They want all the Tesla stuff. I need to call Mr. Dennis and give him the good news. They want to do this ASAP. We need to get everything cataloged and ready to move."

☆ ✩ ☆

Vincent pulled the pillow from his head and heard the knocking again. "Go away!" he yelled toward the bedroom door.

"It's me," Stella said. "Can I come in?"

"I don't care." Vincent rolled over and placed the pillow back on his head.

"Are you okay?"

"I'm fine," he muttered.

"Are you sure?"

"Yes!"

"What happened?" Stella asked.

Vincent sat up in bed. "I don't know. I really don't know. One minute I'm looking at this painting and the next minute everything went weird and I'm lying on the ground."

"Did you see anything? Was it an idea?

"No," Vincent said. "At least, I don't think so. Something was happening, though. But then it all stopped. And I guess I must have accidentally touched the painting."

"Yeah, I heard," Stella said, smiling.

"He's pretty mad, huh?"

"He'll be okay."

"You know, it was really weird. I was looking at this Dalí painting, and all of a sudden it starts to grow these legs. Or stilts. They were kind of—" Vincent stopped talking and jumped up out of bed. He pulled Howard's tie from his pocket. "Oh, man. Stella, I think this was it. I think the watches were changing into this." Vincent pointed to the tower on Howard's tie.

"Watches? What watches?"

"The melting watches in Dalí's painting. Ah, never mind the watches." Vincent started flipping through one of the Tesla notebooks Howard had sent him.

"Look here!" Vincent pointed to some legs that disappeared behind one of Anna's purple daisies.

"Yeah?" Stella sounded confused.

Vincent flipped the page to another drawing. "Here, look here," he said as he held the tie up next to the drawing. "You see this leg here?" He pointed to some sketched lines that disappeared behind a monkey.

"Yeah?"

"Well it's hard to see under Anna's drawings, but I think the device in these sketches is the same as the device on Howard's tie. And the same device I started to see at the museum tonight."

"Oh, yeah," Stella said slowly, looking at the drawing carefully. "I think you're right. But what is it?"

"Call me crazy, but that thing kind of looks like Wardenclyffe Tower."

"What is a Wardenclyffe Tower?" Stella asked.

"A giant tower Tesla built out on Long Island. He never really said what it did, but he claimed it had some sort of amazing powers. They tore it down shortly after he died. They were afraid it was some sort of weapon. A death ray, or something."

"So you think Howard drew the Long Island tower on this tie?"

"No. The Wardenclyffe Tower had a massive building at the base of it. Look at this drawing." Vincent pointed to the monkey sketch.

"No building," Stella said.

"Right. And no building on the tie either. I think this is some sort of device that acted like the Wardenclyffe Tower. Or maybe a model of the tower. Remember how I ran into Howard the night before the contest?"

"Yeah. You said you talked to him in his private museum."

"Right, the Room of Firsts. There's a big curtain hanging from the ceiling in the Room of Firsts and I asked Howard what was behind the curtain."

"What did he say?" Stella interrupted.

"He said it was one of Tesla's greatest and most misunderstood inventions. He said he was hoping that he and I would get a chance to work on it together. I bet that's what Howard was working on. I bet he was trying to build a scale replica of Tesla's Wardenclyffe Tower."

"What do you think the tower does?" Stella asked.

"I don't know. But I almost peeked behind the curtain on my first day at Whizzer. I'll bet we find a tower just like this one behind the curtain tomorrow," Vincent said as he looked down at Mr. Whiz's hand-painted tie.

"Oh, Vincent. I heard your dad talking to Mr. D on the phone. Some museum wants to buy all the Tesla stuff. It sounds like they're moving it all right away."

"Well, we'll have to beat them to it." Vincent pushed the tie back in his pocket. "We just have to get there before they do."

UP EARLY

32

"Stella? Stella? Wake up," Vincent said,
poking Stella in the shoulder. "Wake up."

Stella sat up quickly and banged her head on a table
of salt and pepper shakers. "Ouch!"

"Sshhh. You'll wake someone."

"What time is it? You're wearing the same clothes.
Did you sleep at all last night?"

"It's 4:29. Sshhh, come on. Let's go before Aunt Bonnie wakes up." Vincent tiptoed toward the door.

"How are we going to get there?" Stella asked.

"We'll grab a cab. Now sshh, you'll wake everyone up."

Vincent and Stella stood in from of the Carlisle.

"How are we going to get in?" Stella asked.

"Calli gave me a key," Vincent said.

"I'm not sure about this, Vincent."

"It'll be fine," Vincent said as he opened the door. "The Room of Firsts is on the second floor."

Vincent and Stella climbed the grand staircase and walked down the hallway.

"What are you going to do with the tower?" Stella asked.

Vincent pulled out a bunch of sketches that he had

cut apart and taped together. "I think I finally understand what Howard was trying to do. You see?" Vincent pointed to several shapes taped under a drawing of the tower. "It's all related. The tower, the Tesla stuff we saw at the Met, even my windless kite. They're all connected. They're all pieces of Tesla's brilliant plan."

"Your kite was part of Tesla's brilliant plan?" Stella asked, skeptically.

"No. Not my actual kite, but the high voltage that powered it. I just need to convince Mr. D that Howard was close to discovering something. Something great."

"Wow!" Stella said as they entered the Room of Firsts.

"Yeah. Pretty cool, huh?" Vincent looked up and saw that the Tesla artifacts that had been behind the velvet rope were gone. "Oh, no!" He ran to the large red velvet curtain hanging from the ceiling. He pushed it out of the way. Nothing. "It's gone! It's all gone! Come on, Stella!"

Vincent ran out of the room. Stella chased after and caught up with him at the elevator. They got in and Vincent pushed the sixth-floor button several times. Stella didn't say a word. She didn't know what to say.

The elevator door opened at the sixth floor and Vincent jumped out and ran down the hallway to Howard's private lab. "NO! NO! NO!" he yelled.

"What is it?" Stella asked as she ran into the empty room, out of breath.

"It's gone! It's all gone! All the Tesla stuff is gone!"

The room was empty. The only evidence of the Tesla inventions were the stains on the cement floor. The walls were bare and all of Howard's toy prototypes had been neatly placed in boxes next to the door.

"Unbelievable!" Vincent paced the empty room.

"They might be over at the Met," Stella offered.

"What?"

"The Tesla stuff. It might be over at the Met. Your dad said something about cataloging and packing them ASAP. Maybe they moved the stuff last night?"

"Yes! I bet you're right!" Vincent grabbed one of the boxes of toys. "Come on, Stella. Grab a box. We don't have much time."

"Well, well, well. Good morning, Vincent," the guard said. "Where's your Aunt Bonnie?"

"Ah, she's on her way. We're supposed to take this stuff downstairs and put it with the other stuff," Vincent said, lifting up the box of toys for Mr. Wooler to see. Vincent hoped Stella was right and that the Tesla collection was indeed in the basement of the Met and not on its way to the Museum of Modern Art.

"Oh, yeah," the guard said, holding the door open. "Go on down. You know the way, right, Vincent?"

"Yes. Thanks, Mr. Wooler." Vincent and Stella headed for the stairs and hurried to the basement. They walked down a long hallway and entered a large room.

"It's kind of déjà vu, isn't it?" Stella asked as they walked into the basement room full of Tesla inventions.

"Yeah . . . Look, Stella!" Vincent pointed to a five-foot tower in the far corner of the room. It had six white wooden legs and a shiny metal hemisphere on the top.

"You were right, Vincent." They set the boxes of toys on the floor. "What do we do now?"

"First, we need to find the vacuum tube Tesla coil."

"What does it look like?" Stella asked.

"It looks like this." Vincent showed her the sketch he had taped to the tower drawing.

"Hey, this part here kind of looks like that thing that

shocked me last time we were down here," Stella said, pointing to the sketch.

"It is the thing that shocked you last time. But it will have more parts on it now. Howard was able to finish it."

Vincent and Stella walked up and down the rows of inventions. Vincent couldn't believe all the stuff Howard had managed to collect. There must have been over five hundred inventions in the room. "It's hard to imagine one person could've built all of this," Vincent said.

"Here it is, Vincent!" Stella bent down and touched the Tesla coil. "The handle is gone, but I remember these plates."

Vincent ran to Stella. "Yeah, that's it all right. Let's get it over to the tower." They carefully carried the device to the tower at the far end of the room.

"Now we just need to find this part." Vincent pointed to the sketch of a long skinny tube with holes drilled in it.

"What is it?" Stella asked.

"I'm not one hundred percent sure, but it might be part of Tesla's turbine tube. I think Tesla used it to connect the vacuum tube coil to the tower. But Anna's monkey is in the way, so I can't say for sure."

"OH, THERE YOU ARE!" Aunt Bonnie said, entering the room. "John said you were down here. Everyone is worried sick about you two. You can't just go running off like that without telling someone. Good heavens, Vincent! You scared us half to death."

"I'm sorry, Aunt Bonnie. I just wanted to get an early start and I didn't want to wake anyone."

"Well, I'll go upstairs and let your dad know you're okay," Bonnie turned toward the door.

"My dad? He's here?" Vincent's voice cracked.

"Yes. They're all upstairs waiting to meet some gentleman about all of this stuff. And they're worried sick about you, Vincent. Your dad feels awful about yelling at you last night. I'll go get him. He's going to be so relieved." Aunt Bonnie walked out of the room.

"We're so dead, Vincent."

"Come on, Stella. We've got to find that tube."

"They'll be down here any minute! Just tell Mr. D about your secret lab and we'll save Whizzer that way."

"No way, Stella. Everyone will go on thinking Mr. Whiz was crazy at the end of his life. Just like Tesla. We can do this. I have to do this."

"Okay."

Vincent and Stella started running up and down the aisles of inventions looking for the tube with the holes.

"There is too much stuff. It all looks the same," Stella said. "How big is this tube we're looking for?"

"I don't know." Vincent was crawling on the ground looking under several tall machines. "Maybe two or three feet? I told you, Anna's monkey is blocking the sketch, so it's impossible to say."

"Could it be this?" Stella held up a narrow metal tube.

"No. It will have holes in it."

Stella dropped the tube and it clanked as it hit the floor.

"Careful, Stella. They're going to hear us."

"Sorry, but I'm a little nervous right now."

Vincent stood up. "Maybe if you start on that side of the room, and I start over there, we can—"

"Is this it?" Stella interrupted, lifting a three foot tube with holes in it.

"I think that's it."

They both ran to the far end of the room to see if they were right.

Vincent bent down at the

base of the tower and handed Stella a cord. "Here, can you plug this in?"

Stella looked at the old cord. "Are you sure this is safe? This thing has to be a hundred years old."

Vincent pointed to the electrical outlet in the wall. "Tesla invented the alternating current that comes out of that wall. And it hasn't changed—"

Vincent stopped. He could hear his dad's voice in the hallway. He looked back at Stella. "Just trust me."

Stella reached down and plugged in the cord.

"Help me slide this in." Vincent raised the metal tube over the top of the tower and lowered it down as Stella guided the tube into the Tesla coil.

"A perfect fit," she said.

"The straps!" Vincent pulled out his sketch. "Tesla had straps on the tower to keep the tube from touching the sides. There are no straps!"

"Vincent? What happened to you this morning? What

are you two doing here?" Norton asked as he walked into the room with Mr. Dennis, Calli, Royal, Earl, Fayman, Mr. Jilliver, and a man Vincent didn't recognize.

"Oh, hey, Dad."

The group crossed the room.

"Wow, you weren't kidding, Norton, there is a ton of great-looking stuff," the man in the dark suit said.

"Mr. Jilliver. Mr. Whitworth. This is my son Vincent and my daughter Stella. Mr. Whitworth is the director of the Museum of Modern Art. Mr. Jilliver is the director of the Met. And, of course, you two know everyone else."

"Ah! So you're the one who caused all the commotion at my museum last night." Mr. Whitworth's voice echoed through the room.

"Yes, sir. Sorry about that."

"Yes. Vincent has very bad migraines that can actually make him lose his balance," Norton interjected.

"Oh, I'm sorry to hear that."

"Yes. Well, they've been better lately. Haven't they, champ?"

"Norton, what are your kids doing here?" Mr. Jilliver interrupted.

"Ah, I'm not sure. What's going on, guys?"

"Vincent just wanted to show me all this cool stuff. You know, before it was gone," Stella said. "Well, speaking of gone. We should get going, Vincent." Stella started walking toward the door. Vincent followed.

"Well, as you can see, it is a formidable collection," Mr. Jilliver said.

Vincent stopped at the door.

Stella whispered, "Come on, Vincent. Let's get out of here."

"No. I can do this." Vincent bent down and picked up one of the boxes of toys from Howard's lab.

"Well, I know this is going to sound strange," Vincent said, walking back toward the group. "But I think I know what Howard was working on when he died."

Vincent set the box of toys down in front of Mr. Dennis.

"Oh?" Mr. Dennis said.

"What is he talking about? We don't have time for this, Norton," Mr. Jilliver said.

"Vincent, I don't think this is the right time or place for this. Let's talk about this later, okay, buddy?" Norton said, with an uneasy laugh.

"No, Dad." Vincent put his hand on the tower. "Later it will be too late."

"PLEASE, DO NOT TOUCH THAT!" Mr. Jilliver scolded. "That is part of a very expensive and very important collection, young man."

"I know what this is. And I think I know what it does. Please, Dad! You have to believe me."

"Vincent, ahh, was very fond of Howard Whiz. And of Nikola Tesla," Norton tried to explain.

"I see," Mr. Whitworth said.

Vincent turned to Mr. Dennis. "I really think I can make this work." Vincent sounded desperate as he motioned to the tower. "The vacuum tube Tesla coil and this turbine tube are all part of it. They seem unrelated, but I believe they're all part of Tesla's great invention. Mr. Whiz had all the right pieces. He just hadn't put them together the right way. Yet. I really think it will work, Mr. D."

Mr. Dennis looked down and noticed that the cord was plugged into the wall. "You really think it will work?"

"Good heavens! You haven't been playing with this— have you?" Mr. Jilliver asked. "Norton, please! This is extremely inappropriate!"

"I'm sorry, Mr. Jilliver. I'm sorry, Mr. Whitworth,"

Norton said. "This has been a difficult week for every-one. Please, Vincent! Let's go!"

"No, wait a minute." Mr. Dennis raised his hand. "I still own all this stuff, right? Go ahead, Vincent. Let's see if it works."

"WHAT?" Mr. Whitworth exclaimed. "I'm not buy-ing that if he wrecks it! NORTON! PLEASE CONTROL YOUR CHILDREN! THIS ENTIRE PLACE COULD GO UP IN FLAMES! WE DON'T KNOW IF—"

"Oh, quiet down," Royal interrupted. "Let the kid try. Go ahead, Vincent, flip the switch."

"Well, I can't. Not right now," Vincent said. "It's miss-ing the straps." He motioned to where the straps should have been on the tower.

Mr. Jilliver threw his arms up in disgust.

"Mr. Shadow. Have I taught you nothing?" Mr. Den-nis asked.

"Pop-Tarts," Stella said, looking around the room. "It's like the Pop-Tarts. What else could be a strap?"

"Pop-Tarts?" Mr. Jilliver said. "I give up."

Vincent reached in his pocket and pulled out Howard's tie.

"Thattaboy, Vincent." Mr. Dennis smiled and repeated, "Thatta boy!"

"Would someone please tell me what is going on around here?" Mr. Jilliver demanded.

"OH, CAN IT, GEORGE!" Norton said. "And let my son concentrate."

Vincent used Howard's tie to secure the turbine tube in the middle of the tower. He bent down next to the vacuum tube Tesla coil and looked up at Stella. "Ready?"

"Ready." She smiled.

Vincent flipped the on switch. The tower hissed and the turbine tube started to glow. Sparks leaped from the metal hemisphere. Everyone stepped backward.

"Happy now?" Mr. Jilliver said. "Nothing. It does nothing. Just like the rest of this junk."

"Well, I don't think I would call *that* nothing." Vincent pointed to the rows of Tesla inventions.

Row after row of the inventions started spinning, grinding, buzzing, and shaking.

Multicolored lights were now coming from inside the boxes of toys at Mr. Dennis's feet. The box began to shake violently.

"Good God!" Royal yelled over the noise. "What is going on?"

The box tipped over and a doll crawled out. Then a bouncing ball.

Norton yelled something as a yellow-and-black toy bumblebee buzzed past his head, leaving a trail of bubbles behind.

"Well, I'll be," Fayman said.

Smoke started pouring out of several Tesla inventions. Vincent bent down and pulled the power cord from the wall and the room went silent.

"What was that?" Norton asked.

"Unless I'm mistaken, I'm guessing that was high voltage!" Mr. Dennis said.

"Yup," Vincent said. "Wireless power! First invented and demonstrated by Tesla in 1893!"

"And all those toys back at Whizzer? All the ones with no batteries? They're all real? They all work?" Royal asked.

"Yup." Vincent was beaming.

"So that is what Howard was working on all that time," Calli said. "We have more than enough toys for a new Wondrous Whizzer Wishbook!"

"Yes," Vincent said.

"You never cease to amaze me, Mr. Shadow!"

"Oh, no. It wasn't me, Mr. D. This was all Howard," Vincent said.

"And Tesla," Fayman added. "Boy, do I owe that guy an apology."

"Well, I'm not sure what just happened," Norton said. "But I'm guessing the Tesla inventions are no longer for sale, right?"

"Right you are! Sorry for wasting your time this morning, Mr. Whitworth, but it looks like I have a toy company to run."

"With more than enough toys to give that rat Spinowski a run for his money," Earl added.

"Oh yeah," Vincent said, turning to Mr. Dennis. "About that rat Spinowski. Dad, you may want to sit down for this one. . . ."

A WISH COME TRUE

34

"Kent Bloomingtrip here reporting live from the Whizzer Toy Company. With me today is Vincent Shadow. Now, Vincent, you were the winner of this year's Whizzer Toys contest. Is that correct?" Kent asked, holding the microphone up to Vincent's mouth.

"Yes."

"And remind the viewers, what was your winning toy invention?" Kent asked.

"Ah, they were bubbles that carried sound. I call them Pop Tunz," Vincent said.

"Fantastic!" Kent said, looking directly into the camera. "Well, folks, it turns out that young Vincent here has invented more than just those winning bubbles. If the viewers at home will recall, I did a story a few months ago about a young toy-inventing phenom named Timmy Zimmerman. Timmy had claimed to be the inventor of a bunch of toys that he had sold to the Spinowski Toy Company.

"Turns out that young Timmy had fooled us all! Even this seasoned reporter! A judge has ruled that all of the inventions Timmy claimed to have invented were actually invented by Vincent." Kent looked down at Vincent. "I guess that makes you the young phenom toy inventor, doesn't it?"

"I guess so." Vincent smiled.

"Well, Vincent. Now that you have your toys back, what are you planning to do with them?"

"Most of them will be part of the new Wondrous Whizzer Wishbook," Vincent said.

"How exciting! I remember how much I loved the Wishbook when I was your age. When will the new Wishbook be out?" Kent asked.

"We're hoping to have it out by the holidays," Vincent said.

"And I've heard rumors that the new Whizzer toys won't even need batteries. Is there any truth to that?" Kent sounded skeptical as he held the microphone up to Vincent.

"That's right. Most of the new toys won't require batteries," Vincent said confidently.

"How is that possible?"

"Howard G. Whiz was working on a new kind of wireless power when he died. It was actually first created by Nikola Tesla over one hundred years ago. It's pretty cool stuff."

"I'll say it is. So what will these wireless toys do?" Kent asked.

"Lots of things. There are glasses that let you see the world in cartoons. A device called the Whizzer Word Caster that lets you throw your voice . . . in up to six different languages. Uncatchable footballs. Puppets that interact with each other. Even a logrolling game!" Vincent said. "It's going to be awesome!"

"Wow! That definitely sounds like a Wishbook not to be missed," Kent said, stepping toward the camera. "Well, you heard it here first, people. You can expect to see some amazing things from Vincent Shadow and Whizzer Toys this fall.

"For Action One News, this is Kent Bloomingtrip saying good-bye for now."

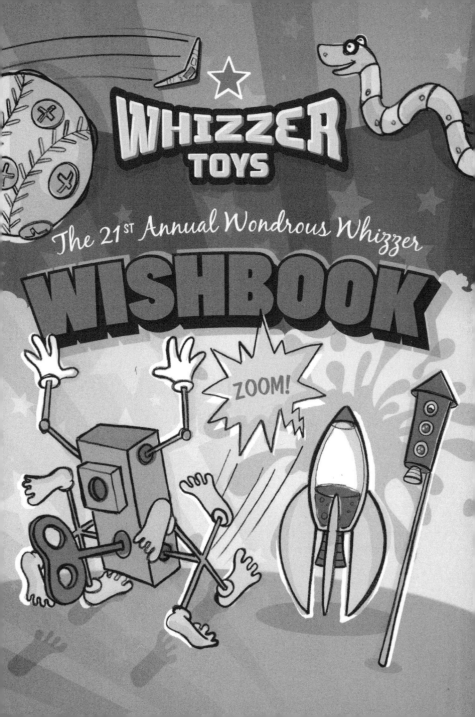

The 21st Annual Wondrous Whizzer
WISHBOOK

Dear Reader,

In addition to introducing all our magical new toys and games, this issue of the Wishbook provides a sneak peek at our upcoming Whizzer Power Tower. We believe the Power Tower will change the future of toys forever.

From your friends at

Table of Contents

Water Crackerz &
Water Rocketz
page 6

Cartoon-O-Vision
Glasses
page 11

Pop Tunz
page 14

Screw Ballz

Strike 'em out with the new Whizzer Screw Ballz. Simply turn the screw heads to change your pitch. It has never been easier to throw a slider, curveball, changeup, and even the dreaded knuckleball. Screw Ballz feature cork and rubber centers, are covered in full-grain leather, and are baseball-size. Batter up!

Belching Bob

How loud do you make a belching toy? Our engineers had no idea, so they decided to put Belching Bob to the test. We gathered a group of mothers and increased the belching volume until everyone was 100% in agreement that Belching Bob was the foulest, most obnoxious toy they had ever seen. That's when we knew we had it right!

DISGUSTING!

Fun Fang Straws

With their frightening fang design and double-straw pumping power, drinking a glass of your favorite beverage has never been more exciting. Fun Fang Straws are dishwasher safe and reusable. Hope you're thirsty!

Crazy Jack's Logrolling Game

Crazy Jack Johnson is a seven-time world champion logroller. And now you can roll like Jack, too. Crazy Jack's Logrolling Game features a solid propylene log core and a milled-bark-textured surface for optimal grip. Just like the logs Crazy Jack rolls!

FUMBLE FUMBLE
Football

Yes, the other team
fumbled the ball again.
And again. And again.
But not your team.
Because you know
the secret behind the
new Whizzer Fumble
Fumble Football. It's
sure to be a long day
for the other team....

UNCATCHABLE!

TRICK *your friends!*

WATER CRACKERZ & WATER ROCKETZ

The Whizzer Toy Company is proud to introduce the world's first fireless fireworks. These water-powered pyrotechnics provide massive H_2O payloads and pack quite a punch. Drench the competition with Skyrockets, Water Crackerz, and Roman Water Sticks.

Roman Water Sticks

Water Crackerz

Wet & Wild!

Skyrockets

Whizzer Trash Talkers

Whizzer Trash Talkers are never at a loss for words. Simply open the lid and the Trash Talkers start talking. Trash Talkers run on two AA batteries and come preprogrammed to hurl insults in five languages.

Trash Talkers feature four different trash-talking levels:

1. Mildly Annoying
2. Somewhat Insulting
3. Fairly Offensive
4. Downright Rude

SKETCH FX

You won't believe your eyes (or ears) when you sketch with Whizzer's Sketch FX. These amazing markers contain advanced movement sensors that recognize over 100,000 different shapes and help bring your drawings to life. Now, when you draw a cow, you will not only see the cow, but hear it moo! Simply slide your existing marker into the Sketch FX unit and begin sketching.

MOOO!

FEATURES ADVANCED MOVEMENT SENSORS!

Scratch & Sniff Paints

Art has never smelled so good! With a quick scratch of the paint, your green grass smells like fresh-cut grass. Your red campfire smells like a blazing fire. And your pink pig smells like, well, a pig.

Yo-Tunes

Many instruments use strings to make music, but never quite like this! Control the tone, pitch, and tempo with a flick of the wrist. Yo-Tunes feature fifteen different instruments. Grab your friends and rock out!

YO, YO, HERE WE GO!

CARTOON-O-VISION Glasses

YOU WON'T BELIEVE YOUR EYES!

See the world in full-color 2-D graphics. These glasses use advanced vector optical lenses to render your entire world in cartoonlike animation. Now you — or your dog — can be the star of your own animated world!

Whizzer Windupz &
Whizzer Windupz Wall Walkerz

This classic favorite is new and improved! Whizzer Windupz have been part of the Wondrous Whizzer Wishbook for over 20 years. And they keep getting better! We're proud to introduce Wall Walkerz to the classic Whizzer Windupz family. Now the fun doesn't have to stop just because the room does!

FAIRY FEATHER PRINCESSES

These magic little pixies come from the Kingdom of Quail. Back home, Jada, Mercy, Sona, Flare, and Tyna are sky princesses. These sturdy little dolls weigh only 0.5 oz each. With a puff of air, the Fairy Feather Princesses will take flight and soar through the air for up to eight minutes. Collect them all now!

COLLECT all 5!

NEW!

SUPER-DUPER!

Pop Tunz

We are pleased to announce that eleven-year-old Vincent Shadow is the winner of last year's toy invention contest for his Pop Tunz creation. Using amazingly advanced high-voltage technologies, Pop Tunz allow you to record sounds and music in bubbles. Unbelievable!

Congratulations, Vincent!

FUN FOR GIRLS and BOYS!

Prickly Pete's Porcupine Challenge

Be careful not to upset Pete or he'll send quills flying! It takes a steady hand and a little luck to remove one of Pete's quills. Whoever removes the most quills without upsetting Pete wins!

Whizzer iBOOMERZ

IMPRESS YOUR FRIENDS!

This is definitely not your dad's boomerang! This fully programmable, GPS-enabled boomerang features an onboard computer navigation system and a built-in 10-megapixel camera. Simply set your course, speed, and height, and let it rip! But don't go anywhere, because your Whizzer iBoomerz is coming back soon…guaranteed.

100% SAFE and FUN!

Whizzer Wireless
WOW GLOVE!

With the flick of a finger, your plane soars high into the sky. And with a twist of your wrist, your car pulls a 360! Put the power and speed in the palm of your hand with the new Whizzer Wireless Wow Glove. The Wow Glove works with all Whizzer R/C cars, boats, and planes.

Just POINT and GO!

Whizzer Super Bionic Ear

Wow! Did you hear what Mrs. Grossman just said to the principal? Of course not—you're not wearing your Whizzer Super Bionic Ear! You'll never be left out of the conversation when you are! The Whizzer Ear features a high-powered unidirectional microphone that filters out background noise and delivers crystal clear sound over 500 yards away.

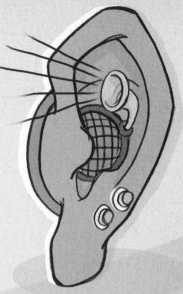

Whizzer Juggle Balls

INCREDIBLE!

Quit clowning around with old-school juggling balls and take your skills to the next level with the new ultra-lightweight Whizzer Juggle Balls. Whizzer Juggle Balls are made from aerogel, first created by Samuel Stephens Kistler in 1931. Aerogel, often called solid smoke, is the lightest and lowest-density solid known to exist in this universe. As you toss them in the air, these balls will defy gravity!

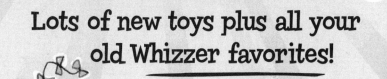

Lots of new toys plus all your old Whizzer favorites!

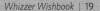

INFLATES TO 10x ORIGINAL SIZE!

Pump-Up Pickup

These little monsters pack quite a punch! Each tire contains a hidden pump to quickly turn your mini truck into a MONSTER TRUCK. This beast can tame the largest obstacles. Shoes, couches, even little brothers are no match for the Pump-Up Pickup.

MIND SKETCH FX

If you can imagine it, you can draw it with Mind Sketch FX. Okay, Mind Sketch FX doesn't exactly read your mind, but it will obey your every thought. Advanced cerebral brainwave detectors allow you to control the magnetic sketch pad with a simple thought. Wireless headset works up to 25 feet away. So, start imagining!

WHIZZER
WORD CASTER

Ever want to be in two places at the same time? Now you can! The Whizzer Word Caster allows you to throw your voice over 500 feet. Simply point the Word Caster in the direction you want to throw your voice, pull the trigger, and speak into the microphone. Throw your voice down the hall, upstairs, or even outside.

TRICK your PARENTS!

Super Bubble Bangers

Smash the Bubble Bangers against the ground and they erupt into clouds of bubbles. Use Whizzer Everlasting Bubbles solution for even more bubble-banging fun!

POP!

FUN FOR HOURS!

CONTEST WINNER!

Robotic Hermit Crab!

by Kiernan McAfee

This robotic hermit crab is made of scrap metal and runs on rechargeable batteries. It's like a real pet, except you don't have to feed it. Just don't get it wet!

SOON TO BE A WHIZZER TOY!

GET HER!!

B.I.G. AMMO

BIG sisters are faster nowadays AND a little foam ball is no match for an older brother.

When you are after the BIG GAME — you need to use the B.I.G. Ammo.

This soon-to-be-patented system uses a chemical reaction to quickly inflate the ammo from four inches to four feet!

Your BIG sister will never know what hit her!!

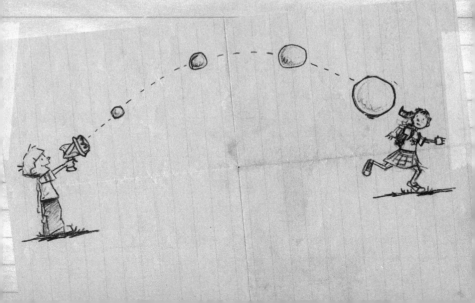

SQUIRT GUN PERMITZ

YOUR ENEMY

Picture This—

You are in a heated battle with friends and you have worked up a mega thirst. You put your squirt gun down and run inside for a glass of water, but when you return you are hit with a massive blast of water—*FROM YOUR OWN SQUIRT GUN!!*

This would never happen if you had a Gun Permitz squirt gun!! Take the gun permit card out and the trigger locks. Only you can use *YOUR* squirt gun!!

MEGA MIDNIGHT GLOW-IN-THE-DARK BUBBLE BLASTER

The fun doesn't have to stop just because the sun sets. Light up your neighborhood with the Mega Midnight Glow-In-The-Dark Bubble Blaster. These amazing bubbles come in six different colors and glow for up to twelve hours.